HOW BLENDED ARE
DUST AND FIRE

Kieran McKendrick

LEGAL STUFF

Copyright © 2013 by Kieran McKendrick
All rights reserved.

ISBN-10: 0988768119
ISBN-13: 978-0-9887681-1-6

Printed in the United States of America

Cover image by Soheil Toosi

www.KieranMcKendrick.com

FOR JULIE AND DON

Geraint

Geraint hooked one end of the rope ladder to the grips on his saddle and let the rest unroll itself until it reached the ground. Once his left foot was well set in a rung near the stirrup, he swung his other stunted leg over the saddle until his entire weight was on the ladder.

Thank the Great Horse he didn't have one of those great hulking Duta'ut horses that were amazing to look at, but useless on the Great Circle where the Dhervina rode. He wondered if he would even survive a fall from something that large. Clambering down, he gathered the reins of his horse and led it to the spring for a drink.

Unlike him, his sister Brys was tall and well formed. She vaulted from her horse easily. She tethered her horse near the spring and handed him a roll of blankets that he knew also contained a change of clothing.

"I'll meet you at the cave," she said. She hoisted a basket with several days of food and water and soon disappeared into the trees despite the weight of the basket.

Geraint had no doubt she would find the cave still musty, damp and unused. He knew he should be more interested, but at this point, he didn't see the need for the cave. After all, it wasn't as if his appearance was all that surprising any longer. The Dhervina had gotten used to him. At least he was pretty sure they had. There hadn't been a problem in over three summers now.

And while he still had to be careful, he suspected that if he simply stayed out of the way, no one would do anything more than give him dark looks. This summer, the most they would do was declare him ostraka, banned from the Dhervina. But he hoped not. It would be hard on his parents and Brys, and he had no idea how he would make his way in the world outside the kereit.

Geraint slipped his horse a treat and made sure it was well secured before slipping the sleeping roll over his shoulder.

Their parents had continued on with the rest of their kereit. It would be several gallops before they could set up their tent at the edge of the Tanaiste. Until then, they would help others set up and earn a few lian. Geraint and his sister would follow and set up the tent after the others were done so as to be certain they were camped on the edge of the kereit so as not to contaminate it.

Geraint felt a quick flash of shame. If not for him, they would be able to set up early and mingle with the other families. He knew his mother was anxious to reconnect with her family and old friends. And, although she didn't voice it, he knew Brys wanted to talk to the other riders. Instead, they had to wait. And all because he had been born a dhavara and was considered ostuda.

Geraint pushed away the unwelcome thoughts. There was nothing he could do.

Except leave.

He didn't want to think about that, either.

Geraint made a face at the steep slope ahead. He was stronger and had grown since last summer, but the prospect of the climb was still unwelcome. But Brys was waiting. He took a deep breath and began the ascent to their hiding place in the cliffs.

Geraint's mind returned to his earlier thoughts as he climbed. It wasn't the first time he had thought about leaving. Now that he was of age, there was nothing to keep him with the Dhervina.

Except his family. *And the horses.* And the knowledge that wherever he went, his deformity would keep him an outcast. At least within the Dhervina he had a home.

And even though he was too small to work with the horses in the way of the Dhervina, he loved them. He could at least groom them and ride them. Besides, he had shown an aptitude for breeding.

If he left, what would he do? He was of little use at anything else.

Geraint stopped for breath under an oaken with thick leaves reaching high above him. The air fell over him like a horse blanket, made heavier by the stillness as it greedily sucked the moisture from his skin. Even the sweat from the horses had dried before he had dismounted.

The shrill buzz of tzettix filled his ears as first one began and then others took up their call.

When he finally moved again, the sound stopped completely.

The rest of the climb was steep and he stopped to rest often, knowing his sister would wait patiently until he could get to the cave. Each time he stopped, the tzettix would resume buzzing, stopping instantly the moment he began to climb. It reminded him of the whispers that followed him whenever he visited some of the other kereits when they met for the important festivals.

At least in his kereit there were fewer whispers.

When he finally reached the cave, Brys was sitting cross-legged near the entrance.

"You're getting faster," she said.

"Doesn't feel like it." Geraint let down the sleeping roll and plopped down next to her. His legs ached from the strain and he was glad the cave wasn't higher up.

"The cave is still safe," she told him.

"Do you think we're likely to need it any longer?"

Brys shrugged. "Not if you're careful. Especially this summer."

"They're used to me now," he said.

"They'll never be used to you," she reminded him sharply. "And this summer you'll be on your own. They'll be watching you closely. You must be especially careful."

Geraint grinned. "I will." He could hardly wait.

"Just remember to stay away from kereit Jedaran. And kereit Oronar. You remember their colors?"

Geraint nodded. "Black and red for kereit Jedaran. Green and brown for kereit Oronar."

"Good. They'll likely set up on the other side of the race course, but they'll be everywhere during the races."

"They won't notice me during the races."

"They might. They are more suspicious than the other Dhervina. As is kereit Jirgin."

"Black and yellow," Geraint said automatically.

"It would be best if you would stay near our kereit," Brys suggested. "At least until the Dheren have met and decided."

"I'm not going to miss the races. Yürki is racing and I want to see how his horse does."

"Just be careful."

"Let's go look at the Tanaiste." Geraint got up and headed for the far side of the cliff.

He was tired of being told to be careful.

The last Tanaiste had been seven summers ago and he had had only six summers at the time. Much too young to understand or enjoy the most important gathering of the Dhervina. Then, as he was not yet of age, he had had to remain in the company of someone who was of age. Which meant he was mostly stuck with his parents.

Now he was finally old enough to go about the Tanaiste by himself and he was determined to enjoy everything about the gathering. It wouldn't be the same if his parents were with him. Or his sister.

There were too many places they wouldn't think of going.

The valley of the Tanaiste was a huge flat plain surrounded by mountains on all four sides with long narrow passes from the south, west and north. The kereits of Kypchak Alshyn which roamed the lands to the west, entered through either the northern or southern passes depending on where the kereits of that kypchak were when they began their journey to the Tanaiste.

The narrow pass from the south was where his kereit and the other kereits of Kypchak Kishyn entered. He could see their colors as they streamed through the pass into the wide plain. Even though they were the fewest in number, there were still hundreds making their way through the pass.

For this was the Tanaiste. The gathering when decisions affecting all kereits of all the kypchaks were made. Deals were made or finalized at the Tanaiste. Alliances made or broken. Feuds settled. Judgments decided.

All of the Dheren, the law givers, would be here and would decide on the fate of serious law breakers. The Dheren attached to each kereit decided the lesser offenses when they occurred, but now they would confer and make sure their decisions had been proper for all Dhervina.

More importantly for Geraint, they would make the final decision about those who had come of age since the last Tanaiste.

Geraint knew far too well the fear that came waiting for the final decision of the Dheren at the Tanaiste. Everyone in the kereit could report on all Geraint's actions over the past summers to the entire Tanaiste. Particularly this past summer.

But not just his actions. Even suppositions or assumptions were heard. Then they would decide if he should be welcome as a full member of the Dhervina.

Should they decide otherwise, the sentence could be anything from banishment to execution.

And he had little say in any of it.

Still, Geraint had tried hard to be as invisible as possible for the past three summers. His parents had received no complaints. He hoped there would be no difficulty now.

He edged out onto the cliff overlooking the sacred valley of the Tanaiste. Below, the encampment teemed with activity as the Dhervina erected tents and settled their horses, even while more and more kereits from every corner of the world poured in. By the time the sun fell behind Khurtagin, the peak that tethered the western edge of the mountains, the valley would be jammed from one side to the other except for the racing plain stretching down the middle of the encampment from one end all the way to the other.

"Do you see our banners?" Brys had followed him and now pointed to a group of tents flying banners of green and yellow further up the valley.

Geraint gave a quick glance. At least they were well up in the valley and not on the southern end near the pass. That meant there would be more to see and he would have a better view of the races. But he wasn't concerned with his own kereit. He lived with it every day and it was the least interesting thing on the valley floor.

"Where are the Talfryn? Can you see them?" The Talfryn were the best riders of Kypchak Alshyn. Kereit Talfryn roamed so far west that it was said there were no winters and the Dhervina who lived there never left the backs of their horses.

Not even to sleep.

Geraint wanted to watch them race. More importantly, he wanted to visit their camp and see their horses up close. He wanted to ask them questions.

"There they are." Brys was pointing at the far end of the valley.

"The red and gold?"

"Yes."

Geraint's heart sank. It would take all day to walk that far. "I'll have to ride if I'm to get there."

"Why would you go to their camp?" Brys was looking at him as if he had just put a saddle on his head.

"I want to see their horses," he said.

Brys said nothing, but her face spoke volumes to Geraint.

"You think they won't let me anywhere near their horses, don't you," he accused.

"The Talfryn are suspicious of everyone. I doubt they would let even the Great Khagan into their camp," Brys said diplomatically.

"Let alone a dhavara who might be there to bring them ostuda."

Brys nodded. "You might be able to talk to a Talfryn at the next Tanaiste. But please be careful during *this* one. It will be so much easier once you are full Dhervina."

Geraint grimaced.

"There will be plenty to do at this end of the valley," she added. "You'll be able to watch everyone race. Talfryn or Vinadi, or even the Great Khagan if he rides this summer."

"You think he might?"

Brys shrugged. "He raced last time. He's always been the best rider of the Dhervina."

If he could see the Great Khagan race, waiting to visit the Talfryn would not be such a hardship. Geraint abandoned the idea of visiting the Talfryn camp this summer. As Brys said, there were plenty of other things to do. And time enough.

Brys pointed to the entrance to the pass on the valley floor. "We might be able to set up camp now."

Geraint caught her hand as she turned. "Do you really think they will allow me full membership?"

"Why not?"

But Geraint noticed that she didn't look directly at him.

"Because I will always be a dhavara and they will always see me as ostuda."

She knelt and looked him full in the face. "The Dheran have no reason to deny you. Once you are a full member, the Dhervina have to accept you."

"Will you then have the chance to make an alliance?"

Brys pulled away and stood up.

"I thought not," Geraint said. He looked down at the valley as the rest of the Dhervina set up their tents and began preparations for the Tanaiste.

"What if we both left?" Geraint turned and looked up at his sister.

"Left?"

"Yes. Both of us. You might have a chance for a family."

"And do you think you will be accepted by the Duta'ut?"

"I've not been accepted by my own people. What does it matter if no one else does, either?"

"You have the protection of the Dhervina. No one dares harm you when you are with us."

Geraint nodded. He had arrived at that same conclusion every time he tried to figure out what to do.

"What about you?" he asked now. "Don't you want to make an alliance? Have children?"

Brys pursed her lips. "What would we do? We have no skill other than horses. We will always be Dhervina no matter where we go. Any village would know who we are. Anyone along the Great Road. Anywhere we've sold horses or even ridden past. We could never hide it. And they would never accept us. Here is just as good as anywhere. Better. Because here we have the horses. Here we have family."

"So you wouldn't come with me?"

She pulled away. "I can't." She began walking away. "We should get back."

Geraint watched her go, wishing he knew what to do.

She was right, of course. What would either of them do if they left the Dhervina? He still had no answer to that.

He was about to head back down when a terrible itch began at the base of his skull. It felt as if something was burrowing into his brain.

Geraint scratched at the back of his head, but the itch was on the inside and he couldn't reach it.

Wincing, he pressed both hands to his head as hard as he could, hoping it would help. But the itch grew stronger.

Worse, it turned into a low whistle that filled his ears.

Geraint backed away from the cliff slowly, hoping no one below could see or hear him as he tried to get away from whatever was burrowing into his brain.

The itch intensified. As did the sound.

He moaned as he staggered away from the cliff.

The sound and the pain subsided.

Geraint stopped moving.

Tentatively, he took a step towards the path to where his sister was waiting, but neither the sound nor the itch returned.

He turned back to the view of the Tanaiste and took a step forward.

Nothing.

Then another step.

The itch began again.

He stepped backwards and it stopped.

Geraint thought about it for a quick trot, then stepped forward again.

This time when the itch began, he began to hum in the same tone as the sound in his head.

The itch instantly subsided into a low hum.

Geraint stepped forward, drawn back to the activity below. The black and yellow banners of the Jirgin were crossing the valley floor and Geraint found himself being pulled towards them.

Suddenly he was spun around and he stumbled, nearly falling.

"What are you doing!"

His sister's face was like thunder. Alarmed, Geraint tried pulling away. She tightened her grip on his vest, forcing him to stand still.

"You were about to go over the edge."

Geraint turned slowly and looked, horrified when he saw he was only a step away from the edge.

"What if someone saw you? We would have to find a new hiding place. And there isn't time now." She pulled him further away from the cliff before releasing him. "Didn't you hear me calling?"

He shook his head as he straightened his shirt. "No. There was something.... I heard this sound..." Words failed him and he just shook his head again.

"You have to be careful," she reminded him. Her voice sounded thick, as if she were about to cry.

"I'm sorry," he said. "I don't know happened."

Brys stepped back, her eyes narrow and her mouth set.

"This is the last summer," she said. "Please Geraint. *Please.*" She looked over him to the spread of tents beyond. "If not for yourself, be cautious for me."

Geraint suddenly felt hollow as he stared at her. What wasn't she telling him?

Finally she returned her attention to him. "We should be able to set up our tent now." But she didn't move. She just stood, watching.

A faint breeze fanned her hair. The tiny bells woven into her hair flashed in the sun.

Geraint hadn't seen it before, but suddenly he could see that his sister was truly beautiful.

His heart ached as he realized what his presence had meant for her.

He *should* leave the Dhervina once the Tanaiste was over. Maybe then she would have a chance.

Geraint looked back at the valley and scanned it one last time. But whatever had been there was now gone.

"Geraint!"

His sister's voice reminded him that they still had to set up their tent, see to the horses, and have everything ready by the time their parents returned.

He would think about what to do later.

SEREN

Even before she opened the ornate box that held her portion of the Great Crystal of the Dhervina, Seren felt the crystal awaken.

She was on the far side of the tent and the unexpected vibration of the crystal caused her to look over at the box in surprise. Her normal practice was to wait for the tent to be prepared and then activate the crystal to clear the space of negative influences. She would then send the necessary vibrations to the Dhervina in this part of the valley. It reinforced the law of no conflict that was required at the Tanaiste, the most sacred gathering of the Dhervina.

The Dhervina were not the most peaceful of peoples and it often took very little for tempers to flare or for someone to pull out a shirka. So she took the opening ceremony with the crystal seriously.

But she had always activated the crystal herself. The crystal had never activated on its own.

At least not as long as she had been its Guardian.

Seren crossed to the crystal and picked up the box. The crystal continued to vibrate and she carried it to the center of the tent.

Her tent had just been erected and her handmaidens bustled around her as they unpacked baskets and made the tent comfortable. The place of honor, as always, had been the first to be set up once the layers of carpets were in place. Around her, the women worked quietly as they finished setting up the tent. They had been trained to move silently so as not to distract her at any time. Normally she was able to block out their movements and the soft hiss of their feet on the thick carpets. But this time, she found it difficult to focus on the energy of the crystal.

"Silence," she commanded.

The handmaidens stopped where they were and sank to the floor until she released them.

Seren opened the box using both hands in the proper ritual.

Like the rest of the Great Crystal, her portion was nearly clear with streaks of gold when resting. It was clearly not resting now. It had turned an opaque white and glowed faintly, illuminating Seren's face.

Its vibration was faint, the sound like a low hum. To bring herself into harmony with the crystal, she vocalized a matching tone until the sound diminished and then vanished.

Seren took the crystal out of the box, holding it in both hands as she focused. She sent out her mind to see if she could see who was activating the crystal. But the source was faint and, before she could follow, it vanished.

She waited, her mind open, but the feeling did not return. Gradually the crystal stopped humming and when she opened her eyes, the glow had faded.

The crystal was again quiet.

Seren returned the crystal to the box and closed the lid slowing, wondering who had set it off.

Was the crystal picking up a new Talent?

She had not had the opportunity to train a new Talent in over twenty summers. Crystal talent was extremely rare and Seren had had to read the crystal on her own for much too long. She needed the support of a younger Talent. And when her time came, she would need a suitable replacement. She had been becoming concerned that she might never find a new Guardian for the southern kypchak.

The prospect of a new Talent revitalized her.

It had to be one of the girls who had come of age this summer.

Now that Seren knew there was a possible Talent in the kereit, she must be especially watchful. If she waited too long, the girl could lose her Talent through the lack of training. Or she might take another path away from service as a Guardian. Once a girl pledged her path, even the power of the Guardian was as useful as a lame horse.

The ancient prophecy suddenly came to Seren's mind. It had spoken of this summer as important and had promised the rise of a strong Guardian.

She had never imagined that *she* would be the Guardian to discover the Khevira who would save the Dhervina from their enemies in the summer of the second moon. To have the chance to mold the Great Protector of the Dhervina was a dream beyond measure.

Then Seren brought her thoughts back to the present. She would not be the correct Guardian if she could not govern her own thoughts.

She must be especially diligent these next few sun cycles if she was to find this new Talent.

ANDRAS

"Andras! Come away from there."

Andras was busying himself with the tent decorations while he watched Brys and her accursed brother set up their tent. He had intended to offer his help when he first saw Brys arrive, but no matter how much he wanted to talk to Brys, he wasn't about to get that close to the dhavara.

Around him the other members of his kereit exchanged greetings with relatives and friends as they finished setting up their tents. Gifts of fermented mare's milk and delicacies made the rounds. Normally he would have joined in, but his desire to talk to Brys had eclipsed everything else.

Andras had begun watching for Brys as soon as the colors of kereit Halaka had fluttered into the valley, but Brys and her brother hadn't appeared until all the places for tents had been taken. They had had to make do with a small space nearly rubbing up against the mountain that rose precipitously from the valley floor.

Now, kereit Halaka had nearly finished putting up their tents and settling the horses, but Brys still had much to do and the brother had not yet left.

Andras knew the dhavara was of age this summer. It was all he had thought of since the festival of Makara three turns of the moon since. With the dhavara coming of age, that meant Brys would no longer be forced to watch over him. Andras had thought he might now have a chance to speak with her and persuade her of the benefits of an alliance with him.

Andras watched Brys out of one eye as he hooked the emblem of three stars designating their family onto the tent flap. One of the catches didn't quite fit over the hook and it began to slip.

Andras muttered a curse and turned his full attention back to the emblem. It was ostuda to have the family emblem fall. Especially during the Tanaiste.

Once he was certain it was secure, he took another glance across the way out of the corner of his eye. The dhavara was still bustling around on stunted legs as he helped Brys decorate the tent with the green and yellow colors of their kereit and the family decoration of the crescent moon.

"Leave," Andras muttered, hoping the Great Horse might attach power to his words and urge the dhavara to explore the Tanaiste, giving him a chance with Brys.

But, of course, nothing changed. Andras did not have the power of the crystal to add hooves to his words.

"By the Great Horse, Andras! Now."

His mother yanked at his arm and practically dragged him back into their tent. She was not a tall woman, but she was strong and she faced him now with stern eyes that told him she was about to enmesh him in a serious matter.

He already knew he wanted nothing to do with whatever she had in mind. Worse, she was taking him away from Brys at a most critical time.

"I've spoken to Manan Yorath of kereit Besut of Kypchak Ulshyn. The kypchak of the Great Khagan himself." She patted his cheek to make sure he was paying attention.

"You remember his kereit stopped with ours at the Kharkat festival last summer. Seems you spent a little time with his daughter and now she won't consider anyone else for an alliance."

"No!" Andras tried to pull away, but his mother only tightened her grip on his arm.

"Yes," she hissed. "You cannot make an alliance with that girl." Her eyes flicked to where Brys was taking an ornament from the dhavara and adding it to the tent flap. "The ayna'al in their blood will taint ours and then you and your children will be ostraka. Do you want that?"

Andras shook his head miserably. "There's nothing wrong with Brys."

"If one member of the family is tainted, the whole family shares the stain. The Great Law says this clearly. As does the Council of Dheren. We cannot ally with such a family."

She let his arm go finally and stepped back, her eyes searching his face intently. "You already know this. Had you thought to make her your avesta?"

Andras nodded. "It would be the only way."

She shook her head. "No. There would be little difference in any event. Any spawn of such a family is cursed." Her eyes went back to Brys. "Besides, the girl is unlikely to consider such an arrangement. She is proud, that one."

Her eyes flicked back to Andras. "I suspect she has other plans. She has already accepted her status. Unlike you. It may not be her fault, but no family can take a chance on an alliance with them. No matter how beautiful the girl."

"What do you mean?"

"She is a good rider. Young and strong. She competed well against the riders of kereit Talfryn at the Makara. She will likely become Khutulun."

"No." Andras turned to look at the girl who had so captured his heart three summers earlier. To think of her as Khutulun and untouchable was unbearable.

"At least as Khutulun, she will have a place and the respect she earns in battle or serving the Guardians."

"But what if the dhavara were to leave or be expelled? Would that not lift the ostuda?"

His mother shook her head. "The taint remains. There is no hope in that direction." She took his hand. "Come and meet Eleri. I think you will be pleased."

"Now? Can it not wait a little while longer?"

She let go of his hand. "A few gallops only. It is time you made an alliance. If you become hand-fast at this Tanaiste, then you will spend the summer with kereit Besut in the north getting to know her and impressing her father. If all goes well, we will finalize the alliance at the Kharkat. It will give you the chance to become an important man. Possibly even serve the Great Khagan directly."

Andras couldn't think of a good reason to reject his mother's matchmaking. She would only find another. Besides, if he turned down this one, it might give insult to the other family. Fighting was not allowed at the Tanaiste, but they could easily be ambushed on the way out of the valley. His kereit was small and no match for any kereit from Kypchak Ulshyn. And, as she said, it was the kypchak of the Great Khagan. That could lead him to more horses and power than even his father had amassed.

"Later tonight," he promised. Perhaps by then he could find some way to have Brys for himself.

She patted his shoulder. "Good. We will join them for the evening meal. It will be an excellent alliance." Then she was a whirl of bells and ribbon as she returned to the festivities.

Andras peered around the tent opening to Brys' tent where the dhavara was handing Brys more decorations for the tent. He gritted his teeth. He still didn't understand why kereit Halaka hadn't gotten rid of the dhavara long ago. Maybe if they had ...

He let his thoughts wander to what might have been until finally the dhavara waddled off. Andras started across eagerly, then realized he had forgotten to change out of the drab riding clothes he had worn on the trip to the Tanaiste.

He stopped. *Did he have time to go back and change into something more presentable?*

He looked down at himself. His trousers were grimy from riding and his vest had stains from the meals he had gulped on the way. He couldn't present himself to Brys looking like this.

Andras hurried back inside the tent and dug through the rolls of clothing and blankets the servants had placed in the middle of the tent until they could sort through it all. His good clothes were in there somewhere.

Fortunately, his blanket roll was near the top. He unrolled it next to his sleeping mat and found the black trousers, white shirt and green vest that signaled kereit Malika. His mother had made them for this summer's Tanaiste and no one had yet seen them. Brys would be the first to see how fine he looked.

He hurried back to the opening to make sure Brys was still there.

Just as he looked out, he saw her stride past. She was still wearing her riding clothes, but still looked impossibly beautiful with her long black hair and dark eyes.

Andras put his festival clothes on his sleeping pad and quickly followed. He wasn't sure yet what he was going to say, but there had to be something he could say or do that would make her his.

GERAINT

Geraint had begun to think the tent would never be set up properly. It always took a long time as they weren't wealthy enough for a servant. And as he was so short, Brys had to do a bigger portion of the work.

Finally though, she pinned on the last decoration and released him to explore the fascinations of the Tanaiste for the first time on his own.

Being considered ostuda, Geraint had learned to stay in the shadows and pass unseen. Staying to the side to avoid being trampled was normally second nature, but today it proved more difficult than usual.

Now that he was on his own, there was suddenly so much to see. Much more than he had anticipated. He could go anywhere and do anything. And even though he had been looking forward to this since last summer, he suddenly had no idea of what he was going to do first.

The valley was a whirl of color. A few still wore clothes dusty from the journey, but many had already decked out in festival finery. Open tent flaps revealed others putting the finishing touches on their vests or in their hair. Everyone had something new they had obtained during the last seven summers that they now wanted to show off. One woman had a shawl that she kept tying this way and that. Geraint watched as she finally decided to wear it over one shoulder with a family emblem clipping it in place.

Tents were decorated in the colors of their kereits and glittered with family emblems and other decorations they had obtained on the Great Circle. Most of the tents surrounding him displayed the green of Kypchak Kishyn. But a few bore the red of Kypchak Alshyn which rode to the east. Most were related to one degree or another and this was the time to catch up and reestablish family ties.

The swirling mass of people waving, hugging, and thumping each other on the back with shouts and greetings made Geraint's head spin. Little ones shyly hung behind their parents. Older children, especially those who were now of age were missing from the melee around Geraint. They likely had run off to see the early races or hang around the kereits of Kypchak Orshyn and hear stories of their bloody conquests in the land to the east.

Horses neighed in the shade created for them next to the tents. Bells tied to ribbons on clothing or woven into hair jingled as people jostled by.

Geraint was so busy looking around, that suddenly all he could see was a mass of people and tents and he had no idea where he was.

He took refuge in a patch of shade next to the tent of a leather worker. Hides tooled with elaborate designs stood in front of the tent as an enticement to see what else might lie inside.

Up a little further, a gold and green banner floated in the slight breeze. Geraint knew gold was the color of Kypchak Ulshyn, but didn't know which kereit the green represented.

It was unusual to see a tent belonging to the kypchak of the Great Khagan himself at this end of the valley, let alone set up in the midst of the disdained southern kypchak. They usually stayed together in the center of the valley.

He wanted to ask someone whose it was, but knew better than to ask. It would draw attention to his presence. So far there had been a few black looks, but no one had said anything.

Yet.

Geraint edged further into the shadows so he could listen to the conversations swirling about him. The presence of a tent from the Kypchak Ulshyn likely meant an alliance was being negotiated. Maybe he could glean a little gossip to pass on to his mother. She would love to have a jump on the talk.

But all he heard was questions and wonderings.

That could only mean nothing was decided. It would be a true honor to have an alliance within the Great Khagan's kypchak. As far as he knew, no kereit within Kypchak Kishyn had ever made an alliance with that of the northern kypchak.

Geraint thought about it. It would have to be Andras' family. They were so wealthy that counting their horses was difficult. They even had to camp on the edge of the valley in order to have enough room for all of their horses.

But if Andras had a pending alliance, why would he pretend to work on his tent for so long and moon over his sister? Did he think he could make Brys his avesta?

Geraint grinned. If Andras thought that, he didn't know Brys.

Now that he had an idea of where he was, Geraint made his way towards the gold and green banner to see if he could find out anything more.

He ducked around a group of revelers and crossed the way past the next tent. A woman looked up, startled. She drew back slightly and put up her hand, two fingers extended, in order to ward off ostuda.

Geraint saluted her gravely and kept going. Once past the tent, he ducked into the shadow of the next tent. He peered back briefly. A few looked in his direction, but there were no angry gestures and no one was running after him, so Geraint continued past the tents of his kereit.

After rounding a corner, Geraint saw a group of older boys up ahead and he quickly detoured around a tent with green and red banners and decorated with silver turtles.

He had run into Tegan and his friends before, but had usually been with his parents on those occasions. They were well known for their short tempers and desire to join the Khirgis, the most elite kereit of warriors in the Dhervina. They hadn't had much opportunity to fight in the lands to the south, so they often started fights in some of the towns or with others in the neighboring kereits. It didn't take much to get them excited.

The worst of the lot was Tegan of kereit Merkit.

It wasn't only Geraint he had tried to bully. Tegan and his friends could be counted on to go after anyone younger who might have something they wanted or who just happened to be there when they were angry or wanted something to do.

Geraint had become expert at staying out of their way, but that had not been true of the other boys in his and the neighboring kereits. Only last summer Tegan had dragged Andras behind his horse for over a gallop. It had been only the goodness of the Great Horse that Andras had gotten off with only bruises. As far as Geraint could tell, Tegan had done that only because he had lost a wager on a horse race and Andras had said something about it in Tegan's hearing.

However, Geraint seemed to sense when they were coming and had managed to hide or get to safety in time. Which meant they had so far confined their dislike of him to harsh words, making it clear how they felt about him and his presence in the kereit.

Now that he was on his own, Geraint wouldn't be able to run to anyone for protection. And at this Tanaiste, he didn't want to tempt fate.

A sudden shout sent a chill through Geraint's veins. He looked to his left and saw a small opening. He ducked through and darted into the next tent.

Fortunately, no one was inside and Geraint hurried through and out the other side.

He turned right and stepped into the shadow of the next tent, then melted back as far as he could until his back ran up against something solid.

Hoping he hadn't accidentally run into his would-be tormenters, he turned carefully. Geraint breathed a sigh of relief when he saw it was just a large basket. Better yet, behind it stood a number of other baskets waiting to be unpacked.

ANDRAS

It didn't take long for Andras to be grateful he had not had a chance to change into his festival finery. Tramping feet and passing horses stirred up large puffs of dust and many he passed were already coated with much of that dust. His own clothes, already worn and dirty from the journey here, had added even more dust, turning even his green vest to dull tan. If Brys were to look back now, she would be unable to see him in the crowd of equally dusty Dhervina. Fortunately, she had yet to turn around and he had been able to follow her without difficulty.

Andras' heart grew heavier with each step as Brys continued up the valley. She was indeed going in the direction of the Khutulun. While it was always possible she was going to visit someone else, he suspected his mother was right. *How had she known?*

He pushed the idea out of his head. Brys was likely joining the Khutulun because she had no chance of an alliance. But what if her brother was banished? There might still be an chance.

No matter what his mother thought.

He knew she disapproved, but she would likely come around once the matter was settled.

TEGAN

Tegan and his friends were on their way to watch the early races when Kelmon saw a particularly wicked blade at a stall on the main thoroughfare. It was a new berdysz axe that had been redesigned to be even bigger and more deadly.

Kelmon was extolling the virtues of the blade when Tegan caught just the slightest movement out of the corner of his eye. He turned his head just in time to see the dhavara duck behind a tent.

This was even better than the races.

"Ho! Kelmon, Jolan! The dhavara! He's in there!"

Tegan darted to where he had seen the dhavara, but there was no sign of him and no way to get through.

He ran around to the other side to see if the dhavara had managed to squirm out that way, but saw nothing.

He stood very still and revolved slowly, looking for even the slightest movement.

Jolan and then the others joined him and Tegan signaled them to wait.

"What is it?" Jolan asked.

"It's that cursed dhavara. He's here somewhere. And no one watching him."

"I didn't see him," Kelmon said.

Tegan looked down a narrow passage behind a tent, but all he could see were some storage baskets still full and waiting to be unloaded.

Jolan clapped him on the back. "He's long gone by now," he said.

Tegan wasn't convinced, but there was no sign of the dhavara or which way he might have gone.

Kelmon leaned close. "Leave it for now. The Dheren will be watching and to have trouble at the Tanaiste would truly be ostuda. If the dhavara is to be found and dealt with, the Great Horse will bring him our way."

Tegan looked around one more time and then nodded. "Let's go see the racing. As you say, we can catch him some other time."

As he went, though, he looked back, hoping to catch the dhavara when he emerged from whatever hole he had hidden in.

Brys

Brys made her way quickly towards kereit Khutulun which appeared to be halfway up the valley. She had seen Andras of kereit Malika hovering near his tent ever since she had arrived and she wanted to get away before he had a chance to speak to her.

While he had always been terribly polite, he always looked at her with a longing that made her uncomfortable. After awhile, it was too tiring to be in his presence. He clearly wanted some kind of relationship, but Brys had known for summers that there was no chance of an alliance with him.

Or anyone else, for that matter.

Not that it mattered. She had long since decided that she wanted nothing to do with the tedious duties and obligations that came with an alliance.

Let alone the idea of allowing a male into her bed.

Any male.

Not even if he was a member of one of the wealthiest families of the Kypchak.

In a way, Geraint's unfortunate deformity had been a blessing. It had freed her from feeling as if she had to make an alliance just to satisfy her parents. Now that Geraint was of age, she was free to become Khutulun and gain all the freedom that came with it.

She had worried about having to deal with Andras before she could get away. This summer was terribly important and she could not take the chance of being seen as rude or insulting.

When she saw him approaching after Geraint left, her heart had sunk. He would cost her valuable time. But then he had hurried back into his tent. Probably to change into something more appealing and she had seen her chance.

The moment Andras disappeared behind the tent flap, Brys had brushed the worst of the dust from her clothes, grabbed the gift she wanted to bring to kereit Khutulun and hurried past his tent, making her way quickly up the valley.

She had intended to visit the Talfryn camp, but they had set up so far away that there simply wasn't time. She would have to do that another day.

Today, however, she wanted to greet Idris and speak with the kheran of the Khutulun. Although Idris came from kereit Buriyat, they had become friends as their kereits often traveled together. Many of the families in the two kereits were related to one another so it was a comfortable ride. There was also more safety in numbers. Both their kereits were small compared to some of the others, so it made sense for them to travel together. Several other small kereits had joined them, making it possible to have several Khutulun along for protection.

Idris had become Khutulun just three moon cycles ago. Brys had last spoken to her in Castine when their kereits had stopped to trade and celebrate Makara, the beginning of the season of grass.

Castine was a small village on a wide river with a thriving fish trade. It had become one of Brys' favorite places to stop on the great circle of Kypchak Kishyn. It had been the last major gathering on the way to the Tanaiste and was much less formal than the Tanaiste.

Idris had left for kereit Khutulun as soon as the celebration was over and Brys hadn't had a chance to speak to her since.

Now that all kereits of the Dhervina were assembled for the Tanaiste, Brys wanted to hear everything that Idris had experienced. She also wanted to tell her that she was also going to pledge Khutulun this Tanaiste.

As promised, Idris was waiting for her at the entrance to the Khutulun camp.

The girls greeted each other, but when Idris would have led her inside the encampment, Brys put her hand on Idris' arm to hold her back.

"First, I want to know what it's like," Brys said.

Idris simply shook her head. "I am not allowed to say anything," she said. "You have to speak to the Kheran."

"But she won't tell me what it's like," Brys pointed out. "I know you have only been Khutulun for a short time, but you could tell me what to expect."

Idris shook her head again, the red ribbons catching the sun. "I cannot tell you," she said. "It is either something you are or you are not. My experience as a Khutulun may not be the same as yours. So I am not allowed to say because it could push you to make a decision one way or the other."

"But ..." Brys tried to think of some way to get the information she wanted. "Do you like it?"

"It is right for me," Idris said.

"Do you think it is right for me?" Brys asked.

"I cannot say."

Brys grabbed her friend's wrist and pulled so they were face to face. "Can't you tell me something?"

Maddeningly, Idris simply shook her head yet again. "No."

Brys opened her hand to let Idris free. "But how do I *know*?"

"You will understand if you become Khutulun," Idris said. "Either you are or you are not. That has to be where it begins." She looked at Brys seriously. "Do you want to continue?"

Brys had thought of nothing else for nearly three summers. The freedom. The chance for a life of excitement. The chance to be valued for what she did and who she was. She looked over at the entrance to the Khutulun encampment, then back at Idris.

"I do."

"Then I will take you to someone who can tell you more than I can. But be aware that there are many questions she will not answer as well. In the end only you can decide if you are Khutulun."

ANDRAS

Andras watched miserably as Brys entered the Khutulun encampment. Unlike the other kereits, their encampment had but one entrance. They were one of the most secret kereits of the Dhervina and they protected their privacy ferociously. Andras had even heard of men being ripped to shreds after being caught in a Khutulun camp.

As men were unwelcome in the Khutulun encampment, Andras went over to examine a display of bridles opposite the entrance to the Khutulun camp. He would wait for Brys there. Maybe he could speak to her when she came out.

Around him, people greeted each other and talked excitedly about the races. The air was already heavy with dust and the smells of meat roasting on nearby cook fires. He tried to concentrate on the bridles before him, but while they were carved with all manner of wonderful designs, Andras was too anxious to appreciate them.

The longer Brys remained in the Khutulun camp, the more Andras wanted to do something beyond standing about. Even though there was little he could do, the wait was becoming unbearable.

He saw the owner of the tent watching him and put his hand to his heart to show he had no ill intent.

"You look as if you're waiting for someone to come out of there." The man tilted his head to indicate the camp of the Khutulun.

Andras nodded.

"Once they have made up their minds, there is no going back," the man said, leaning in close and keeping his voice low as if to make sure the Khutulun didn't hear him. "You're better off getting on with your life."

"She hasn't sworn yet," Andras blurted out. "There's still time."

The other man shook his head. "If she has been invited in, then it is already too late. Khutulun is a calling. No man has the ability to stop a woman who has made that choice."

Andras looked back at the entrance to the Khutulun. Still no sign of Brys.

Could it really be too late? He shook his head. He did not believe that.

There had to be something he could do.

The other man shrugged and continued putting out new bridles.

GERAINT

Geraint heard Tegan and his friends leave, but waited a short trot until he was sure they were gone.

Even then, he only raised the lid of the basket slightly to make sure it was clear before clambering out.

When he was certain it was safe, he brushed himself off and returned to the main thoroughfare. He checked again for Tegan and his friends, but they had gone. Even so, Geraint was careful to stay to the side as he continued on.

Just in case.

If it was going to be this precarious at the Tanaiste where all conflict was banned, what would it be like once he left the protection of the valley?

Geraint doubted it would be this dangerous even in the towns of the Duta'ut.

He had grown up knowing that he was barely tolerated. But not until today did he see how much his parents and Brys had shielded him from the worst.

Now that he was of age, he was just beginning to realize how little stood between him and the fear or anger of others.

Geraint wondered how many other in his kereit felt the same as the bullies who had just come after him.

Suddenly the chatter and excitement felt oppressive. The sheen gone, Geraint now saw only the dust and mounds of offal that permeated the encampment. He had never noticed that the traveling clothes that so many still wore, including his own, were filthy.

The glitter that had once seemed to fill the Tanaiste was all a lie.

At least for him.

Perhaps excitement and fun was there for those who belonged.

But he wasn't one of them.

Geraint supposed he had already known that. But now it was more than clear and the knowledge was no longer avoidable.

Geraint steeled himself and started moving forward again. He wanted to get closer to the gold and green tent. Maybe he could cheer his mother up with a bit of fresh news.

He had planned on checking out a few of the horses to see about their breeding, but the idea now felt flat and unappealing.

Instead of inspecting the horses, he would see if he could discover the source of the itch he had felt earlier. He still remembered the black and yellow banner of kereit Jirgin that had been passing by. If they were the source, he would have to be extremely cautious if he hoped to get any answers. They were not known as being either hospitable or helpful.

BRYS

The Khutulun encampment was nothing like Brys had expected.

She had had visions of them practicing with their weapons and honing their fighting skills. But there was none of that. There wasn't actually much of anything to distinguish this encampment from any of the other large family encampments she had seen other than the lack of males.

Like other compounds, the tents faced the center thoroughfare of the Khutulun camp. There were too many tents for it to be perfectly round, so the open area looked more like a fat snake, curved and long. But there weren't nearly as many as Brys expected. In fact, the entire camp felt deserted.

Idris brought her to a tent near the entrance. The flap was open and Idris stepped inside the opening, but did not enter.

"I have brought my friend Brys of kereit Halaka to speak with you," she said.

"Enter in good spirit, Khala Idris," a woman's voice said.

Brys followed Idris into the tent and looked around with surprise.

The inside of the tent was spare. There were none of the furnishings Brys had expected a woman of authority would have. There were barely enough carpets to cover the ground and little in the way of adornment.

"You may go about your duties, Khala Idris," the woman said.

Idris nodded, gave Brys' hand a quick squeeze and departed.

Brys turned her attention back to the other other woman who was eying her as if Brys was a prize mare she was considering purchasing.

Brys stood as tall and straight as possible so the woman would know she was worthy of becoming one of them.

"I am Esyllt," the woman said finally. "I am a Kheran of kereit Khutulun. In my case, I speak with all girls who would be Khutulun. Should you join us, I will also be responsible for you and your training. What questions do you have?"

"Where are all the others?" Brys asked. "I had thought there were many more than I have seen here."

"The Khutulun of Kypchak Ulshyn have an enclave at the north end of the valley. And there is another in the west. Even though this is the Tanaiste, the Dhervina have enemies. So we keep watch. You will also find Khutulun camped near the southern pass.

"I did not see them," Brys said.

"You are not supposed to. But if you become Khutulun, then you will know what to look for."

Brys asked the question that had been on her mind since her friend Idris had become Khutulun.

"How will I know what path to follow once I become Khutulun?"

"You don't," Esyllt said. "First you train. We see what skills you have. What you have a talent for. Then we know where you fit."

"Does that take long?" Brys wanted nothing more than to ride with the scouts like she had seen during the Great Circle.

The other woman smiled. "In times of emergency, we use each Khutulun as quickly as possible. But these are good days and we have time to train and help you become as skilled as possible. There are many things to learn and many ways to serve."

"What do I do?" Brys asked.

Esyllt held up a hand. "We will discuss that shortly. Everything we say here remains between us. Neither you nor I will repeat what we discuss to anyone else. It is also extremely important that you always speak truly. The answers to my questions are not always what you might think. So answering in a way that you think I want to hear could well be the wrong answer. Only the truth is the right answer."

The Kheran studied Brys a hoof beat longer. "Can you answer from your heart?"

"I will do so," Brys promised.

"Is there anyone you're fond of?"

"My brother," Brys said. "But he came of age this summer and my parents are healthy."

Esyllt nodded thoughtfully. "Your brother is a dhavara is he not?"

Brys bit back the anger that flared suddenly.

"He is. What does that have to do with the Khutulun?"

"Nothing," the other woman said mildly. "But once you become Khutulun, we become your family. Your brother will have to fend for himself once you join us."

"I know."

"Are you concerned for him?"

Brys bit her lip. This was one question she did not wish to answer.

"Yes," she admitted after a short hoof beat. "It will be difficult for him, but I cannot always be at his side. He is a man now and must find his own way. And..." Brys wasn't sure she should voice her next thought.

"And?"

"And perhaps one day I will be one of the Khutulun protecting his kereit."

"And should your path go another direction?"

"Then that is what is to be," Brys said. "Perhaps by then he will no longer need such assistance."

"Before we continue, we must first determine whether you are suitable to become Khutulun. This life does not suit all women and when you pledge Khutulun, it is for life. It is not for the uncertain nor can it be tried on like a new vest and then discarded when you discover it no longer fits."

"So I have been told," Brys said. "I have wanted to be Khutulun for three summers and have not changed my mind in all that time."

"Not even for a hoof beat?" Esyllt asked. "Not even when a certain young man from a wealthy family showed his interest?"

Brys flushed. "Especially not then. I have no interest in him. Or any other man."

"You would not have children."

"I do not want any. I have seen childbirth and have no desire to experience that. I do not want to be condemned to chasing after them all day long when I could be on the back of a horse or protecting a kereit from Duta'ut bandits."

Esyllt gestured at her tent with a broad wave. "You will not become wealthy. We often must travel quickly, so we carry little. Even your family has more carpets than I do."

"I can only ride one horse at a time," Brys replied evenly.

Esyllt smiled and nodded.

"You will train in many areas. Not all of them will suit you and there are some things you may not wish to do. But all are necessary. Can you do your best no matter what task is set for you?"

Brys considered the question before answering. "I have had to do many things that I would not have chosen to do," Brys said. "I have never shirked."

"Can you live with cold and hardship?"

"I can." Brys had seldom been cold thanks to her mother's skill in weaving. But they had experienced hardship many times because they did not have the benefit of extra horses or coins.

"Could you rise in the time of darkness and ride for many gallops without complaint?"

"Yes."

"For many sun cycles without rest?"

"Yes."

"Can you obey without question?"

Brys hesitated. She knew she should say yes, but sensed the other woman would know it was not entirely true. She shook her head, eyes down. "Not always."

"Good."

Brys looked up in surprise. Esyllt was smiling.

"The last thing we want is someone who has no mind of her own. You will often be called upon to think for yourself or find your own way to something. You may not always have an elder sister to ask. And if someone should tell you to do something that seems ill-advised, then it is good for all of us that you voice your concerns."

Brys was relieved. "My mother often tells me that I am too outspoken. It is good to know that my words need not always be stifled."

"You may have heard it said that we never leave any Khutulun behind," Esyllt said, her face now taking on a much more serious look. "Can you find the courage to stick by your sisters even if it means your life becomes forfeit?"

Brys had heard this, but still had no easy answer.

"I believe so," she said slowly. "I have never had to test my courage. I would like to think I am that brave, but do not know for certain."

Esyllt didn't say anything, but looked thoughtful. Brys hoped that meant her response was acceptable.

Esyllt stood.

"It is my judgment that you be allowed to make your pledge and become Khutulun. I remind you again that once you commit to be Khutulun, you cannot change your mind. You are Khutulun for life. Are you still willing to do that?"

"Yes," Brys said with no hesitation. She had been dreaming of this for so long that now it felt as if she was in a dream.

The Kheran crossed to a box near the center of the tent. While the box did not have the ornate carving Brys had often seen in other tents, the polished wood shone and looked as if it were glowing red.

Esyllt removed three red ribbons and came to stand in front of Brys.

"Why are you here, Brys of Halaka?" Esyllt asked, her voice taking on a formal tone.

Brys straightened. "I am here to make my pledge to kereit Khutulun," she said, using the words Idris had taught her.

"Do you understand that this pledge is for life?"

"I do."

"Do you understand that we are now your family and must always come before any other?"

"I do."

"Then I welcome you to kereit Khutulun," Esyllt said and wove the three ribbons into Brys' hair, leaving the lower ends free.

"You will meet with Idris and learn the oath," Esyllt told her. "Return at midday in two sun cycles and you will become full Khutulun. You are allowed to change your mind before then only if the circumstances are severe. Do not bring anything with you."

"I understand."

Esyllt gave her another searching look.

Brys didn't know what the other woman saw, but it seemed to be enough because she finally nodded once briskly and led the way out of her tent.

Idris was waiting.

"You will teach Brys the final oath," Esyllt said. "She will return for the ceremony in two sun cycles."

"I understand Kheran."

Esyllt returned to her tent.

Brys grinned at her friend. "So now we are sisters."

Idris kissed her on both cheeks. "Now I can say what I could not before. It is hard, this life. But it is also very good. You will be happy here Brys of Khutulun."

Brys couldn't stop smiling. She finally felt as if she was beginning the life she was meant to live.

ANDRAS

Andras breathed a sign of relief when Brys finally reappeared. Although she was smiling and had red ribbons in her hair, she was not wearing the red cloak of the Khutulun, so it wasn't too late.

He darted forward and took her hand.

"Please don't become Khutulun, Brys. I couldn't bear it if you did."

Brys stared at him and then stepped back, pulling her hand out of his. "Andras of Malika. It is not right for you to take my hand."

"But I want to be your protector. I want you to live in my tent and be with me."

"You would make me your avesta?"

"It is the only way. My family forbids an alliance, but if you were my avesta, you could be with me always."

Brys took another step backwards. She shook her head. "No. I will not be your avesta. Nor anyone else's. It is a position without honor. I become Khutulun in two sun cycles. It is decided."

"Is it because of your brother?" he asked urgently.

"It is my decision," she said.

"But you would consent if it were not for your brother, would you not?" She had to understand what an honor he was offering her. To be accepted despite the ostuda brought by her brother.

"No. I am Khutulun. That is the end of it."

"But you aren't Khutulun yet. I see no cloak or vest or emblem."

"My ribbons declare my pledge. You will see my cloak and emblem by the end of the Tanaiste." She took another step away from him. "I beg you to leave me be. I am honored you would overlook your family's position for me, but it is not to be. I am Khutulun. Now and always."

Andras stared at her. "You will not change your mind? Not for any reason?"

"Not for any reason." She looked at him gravely. "I ask that you let me by."

He held out his hand in one last appeal, but Brys shook her head and walked away.

Andras watched her go, stunned. *How could she not accept his offer?*

"Brys!" He silently begged her to look back. Give him a sign that she would relent. But all he saw was her back until it was swallowed up by the crowds.

GERAINT

Notable on the side of the tent with the gold banner of the Ulshyn Kypchak and the green designation of the kereit was a large jade emblem of a jar pouring out a waterfall of coins. Geraint stopped to admire the craftsmanship of the emblem. The jade in the south was a light green, sometimes almost white. But this jade was a deep green that took his breath away.

He searched his memory, but couldn't come up with the name of the family, although he knew he should know it. Brys would have known. She had a head for learning and seemed to know everything about the Dhervina.

He sidled over to the open tent flap. Someone inside was singing. Hoping the family had already gone to the festivities, he poked his head in to see.

A woman with hair the color of fire was humming an unusual tune as she unpacked a large basket. Geraint gaped for a long trot at the sight. He had never seen hair like that before. It was most amazing. Then, remembering himself, he looked around to see if anyone else was there.

Fortunately, everyone seemed to be elsewhere. The family would likely not want to be questioned about their personal affairs, but a servant might be willing to share a few tidbits.

Geraint stepped into the opening. The servant didn't notice him.

"Greetings." He deliberately kept his voice low to keep from startling her.

She jumped, but didn't drop the blanket she was holding. Even better, she didn't make the sign to ward off ostuda, nor did she run away.

Instead, she looked at him with curiosity. "Are you looking for Manan Yorath?"

Geraint grinned. "No. I was wondering what family has this tent. I am not familiar with the emblem. And since you are camped in the middle of Kypchak Kishyn, I would very much like to know who our new neighbors are."

"You are from the south."

"You can tell?"

She nodded. "Where I come from, we saw many traders from the south."

"Where are you from?"

She perched on a fat cushion. "Mentos," she said. "In the north. But a little to the west so it is not so cold. My people work with iron, so we see many kervans from all corners."

"How long have you been with this family?"

"Since I was captured in a raid eight summers ago."

"Was your home beautiful?"

She grimaced. "It was all black mountains with great dark pits of iron and heaps of slag everywhere. The only green we saw was when the meat went bad." She shook her head at the memory. "It is much better here. Much nicer."

"You don't want to go home?"

"To what? Here I see so much of the world. The family is kind to me. I eat well. There is nothing to go back to."

Geraint wanted to ask her all kinds of questions since she was so willing to talk to him. He particularly wanted to ask her why she was not speaking to him truly. Despite her words, he felt an undercurrent of fear and a great desire to return home. But he knew he could not stay long. It was just a matter of time before someone from the family returned. He did not want to be caught in their tent unasked. So he returned his attention to his reason for visiting.

"Can you tell me, what is the name of the family?" Geraint asked.

"Family Ogedai of kereit Besut, Kypchak Ulshyn."

"Ahh." He tried to sound knowledgeable. "I've heard there is to be an alliance with kereit Malika."

"So it is said," she replied with a shrug. "But they are still talking and the boy has not yet had a meal here."

"And what of the girl?"

"Eleri?" Again the servant shrugged. "She is the one who requested the alliance. She saw the boy during a kervan to the Kholedari festival in the south and has been insistent ever since."

"Then it is fortunate that family Dorben is well-respected for its wealth of horses." Geraint tried to mask his satisfaction. His mother would be most pleased at his success.

"For her? Perhaps. For the family?" Another shrug.

Geraint had another thought. He gave the girl a sharp look. "You aren't afraid of me."

"Should I be?" She looked him up and down. "You aren't pointing any weapons at me. You don't have a sword to my throat. What should I be afraid of?"

"The Dhervina believe I am ostuda."

"Because you are a dhavara?"

He nodded.

"We have many dhavara where I come from," she said. "And there are dhavara on many of the kervans, as well."

"In truth?" The idea stunned Geraint. To think there were others like him in the world filled him with joy. He had thought he was the only one. Perhaps making his way outside the Dhervina would not be so difficult after all.

"In truth," she said.

Geraint heard approaching hoof beats and loud voices. It was likely a good time to be on his way.

"What is your name?" he asked.

"Rhian."

"That's a beautiful name," he said. "May I perhaps speak with you again? I don't often have the chance to speak to anyone."

"Of course."

"I am Geraint of family Tumen, kereit Halaka, Kypchak Kishyn," he told her, giving her his true name. It was the first time he had had the chance to give his designation and, for a moment, he felt bigger and taller than he was.

"I am honored to speak with you Geraint of Halaka."

The loud voices were right outside the tent now.

"Do you have another way out?"

Rhian smiled and pointed to the far left.

Geraint flashed her a grin and quickly made his escape.

Once outside the tent, Geraint quickly moved into the shadows. They were much deeper now that the sun had traveled further to the west. There were few people about now and a roar of voices rose from the center of the camp let him know that most of the Dhervina were at the races. It would be easier now for him to continue up the valley without notice.

ANDRAS

Andras wandered slowly through the Tanaiste, head down. He walked past shirka blades gleaming in the sun and saddles of every design. A myriad of other goods brought from every part of the Dhervina world were laid out for all to see, but the only thing he could see was Brys stepping away from him.

He passed a tent marked with pink ribbons indicating a pleasure tent with women captured on some of the eastern raids. Before the Tanaiste, he had thought a great deal about visiting one of those tents during the festival, but now all desire had ridden away on a horse made of wind.

He knew he should return to his tent and prepare to meet his new family, but that appealed even less than it had earlier.

Andras was just turning to go to the races when he saw the dhavara waddling up the thoroughfare looking as if he was intent on an errand of some sort.

Curiosity piqued, Andras began following.

Perhaps the dhavara was going to show his true colors. Then Andras could get him banned and perhaps then Brys would be his.

Rhian

After Geraint had gone, Rhian wondered who she could ask about him.

She could not ask the family she served. Many Dhervina families treated their captives as family and she knew many who were better off as slaves to the Dhervina than they had been back in their homeland. But that was not true for her.

She knew she should be grateful that she had not been sold to the pleasure tents as many of her friends had been. But her service to her owner was much the same. The only difference was that she only had to service him when she was not assisting the family.

She knew she had been lucky that she had red hair. It was why Yorath had chosen her. Had she been kept by the man who had found her hiding in the mines, she would have been treated much more roughly. She had to remind herself of that on the occasions when Yorath thrust himself into her or beat her when she displeased him.

It could have been much worse. Even so, her only thoughts for the past eight summers had been on how to get away.

Unfortunately, escaping from the Dhervina was not a simple matter. The kereit she traveled with often rode across huge expanses of empty plains. The few times they did get near a town of some sort, it was not large enough to give her shelter. Even larger places would not risk the anger of the Dhervina by hiding a stranger.

But now she finally saw a chance to escape. She had been a new captive when they attended the last Tanaiste. She had been amazed at the wide variety of Dhervina. The ones from the east were even more vicious than those who terrorized her homeland and she had been grateful she had not been captured by one of them.

The Dhervina from the south seemed softer. They spoke more slowly and seemed more friendly. There were also many who had hair and eyes of different colors. Instead of the black hair and black eyes of the other Kypchaks, those from the south often had lighter hair and occasionally she caught sight of eyes the color of the sky such as the boy who had just visited.

She had given much thought to what she had seen seven summers earlier. If she was to have a chance at escape, it would be at the end of the Tanaiste. All she needed was the opportunity to melt into the crowd at the right moment. Yorath, her owner, had many slaves, so she would not be missed while everything was being loaded onto the horses.

At the last Tanaiste, everyone in the valley seemed to depart at the exact same moment. Horses were milling about and people jostled each other in the crush and the cacophony had been deafening.

She had been closely watched at the last Tanaiste because she was newly captured. But even when she had had the chance to escape during their travels, she had not taken it. She had known it would be simple to recapture her and she had seen what happened to the women who tried.

One woman who had been taken shortly after Rhian's capture had tried to escape. She had been a high born woman unused to brutality. So when Yorath had begun breaking her in, she had not understood that it could have been much worse. After only a few visits from him, she had run.

She had left during the night and they had caught her before the morning meal. Then Yorath had given her to his men to use and fight over. By the time they were done, there was little left.

So Rhian had acted the part of a contented servant and bided her time as she waited for the return to the Tanaiste. Now she was no longer watched. At the end of the Tanaiste she would have the chance to slip into the horde of Dhervina going south before Yorath knew she was gone.

Each would think she belonged with another, so when they did reach a town with people who were not Dhervina, she would have no difficulty finding refuge. Then she could take a kervan to some place that never saw the face of a Dhervina.

Now she thought about the dhavara who had visited. She had heard of him. Had caught a glimpse of him last summer when their kereit had been in the south on some errand for the Great Khagan. She had even heard Yorath voice his displeasure that the boy was allowed to remain with the Dhervina. So she knew he was considered an outcast.

She had repeated to him what she told anyone who asked, but he had looked at her in such a way that made her think he knew it was a lie. She did not think he would cause her trouble and the way he had slipped out the back made her think he could be a potential ally.

She would never trust a Dhervina, but perhaps this one was different. It might be worth her time to cultivate a friendship with him.

Once she had seen to the family, Rhian went out to fill the water skins at the stream on the far side of the valley. Many others were already there and Rhian had to wait to dip her skins in the water.

The stream came down from the mountain in a cascade of glittering water that thundered into a large pool before vanishing into a deep chasm. It was an excellent source of water, but there was only a small area where it was safe to pull the water out. Rhian usually had a wait before she could get close enough to dip in her water skins. It was time she craved. It gave her the opportunity to get more information that would help her escape. Dhervina women loved to gossip and Rhian had often found the conversations useful.

As the slave of a wealthy khagan, Rhian could have used one of the cart slaves to haul the water for her, but fetching it herself allowed her to get away from Yorath and his tents for a little while and give herself the illusion of freedom.

It also gave her the opportunity to prove to him that she could be trusted. At least as much as someone like Yorath would ever trust. It would be the key to her final escape. He would never suspect she would not return.

As she was waiting, she turned to the woman next to her.

"I saw a dhavara this afternoon," she said. "I did not know the Dhervina had such among them. Is he of your kereit?"

The other woman spat and made the sign to ward off the ayna'al mati. "No, thank the Great Horse. He is of kereit Halaka."

Another woman leaned in. "They should have killed him at birth. Letting him continue on with the Dhervina was dangerous and foolish."

"Does he cause a lot of trouble, then?" Rhian asked.

"He is ostuda," the first woman said. "All Dhervina know this."

"It is not too late to sew him into his tent and burn it," the second woman said. "It is the only way to rid us of the ostuda he brings."

"But he is just a boy, is he not?" Rhian asked, appalled at the venom in their voices.

"Boy or man, it matters not," the first woman said. "Ostuda is ostuda."

"But this is the Tanaiste," Rhian protested.

"Then ostraka," the second woman said.

Rhian knew that ostraka meant banishment.

"How would he manage?" she asked. "One so young would have difficulty in the world of the Duta'ut."

The second woman shrugged. "No concern of mine. He is ostuda. It is better for all of us if he is no longer here."

"What ostuda has he brought?" Rhian asked. "What did he do?"

The women looked at each other and shrugged.

"Did anyone die? Horses get sick?"

"No," the second woman admitted.

"It matters not," the first woman said. "He is a dhavara. He is ostuda. It will come if he remains."

A third woman who had been listening now leaned in. "The Dheren should destroy the entire family. It is the only way to rid us of the destruction they will bring on our heads."

GERAINT

Geraint stayed in the shadows until he felt the thunder of running horses. The sound vibrated against his feet and filled his blood with a feeling of primitive power. It was the best part of Dhervina gatherings. Even if he left, this he would always remember.

No one would now pay him any heed. Attention was entirely on the races and Geraint walked easily behind the crowds gathered along the race course. Although Tegan and his friends were likely around somewhere, Geraint suspected they were much more taken with the racing than with the idea of catching him.

Still, he kept one eye out for trouble as he looked for kereit Jirgin.

Further ahead, he saw a black banner, but could not see the color designating the kereit. Hoping the kereits of Kypchak Orshyn had camped together, he moved steadily in that direction.

When he got closer, though, he saw the banner was the black and white of a Guardian, not black and yellow. Worse, most of the banners nearby were the red of Kypchak Alshyn. Which meant he had accidentally wandered into the Talfryn and Vinadi camp.

He turned slowly in a circle, hoping to see what he was looking for. There was a sea of color everywhere he looked, but no sign of the colors he was seeking.

"You!"

The voice was loud and too close.

Geraint turned sharply and looked up to see a rider wearing the Talfryn colors.

His heart sank. He had been so watchful for Tegan and his friends that he had forgotten the Talfryn.

"Me?" he asked, hoping the rider was speaking to someone else.

"You. You are a dhavara."

The rider was clearly unsteady. Too much fermented mare's milk judging from the smell of the rider's clothing.

Geraint grinned as cheerfully as he could.

"I am. And you are a great Talfryn rider. I have heard much about the Talfryn riders."

The man looked at him, eyes narrow.

"What are you doing here?" he demanded. "You should not be here. You are ostuda."

Geraint considered disputing that, but knew it was a waste of time. "I am looking for a rider of the Jirgin," Geraint said instead.

"Then you should go to the camp of the Jirgin. They are not here."

"So I see. It is sometimes difficult to see where I am," Geraint said. "Could you tell me which way to go?"

The Talfryn turned to point. As he turned, he caught his foot and tumbled ungracefully to the ground, legs and arms whirling every which way as he fell.

Geraint couldn't help himself and grinned at the spectacle. But he knew immediately that it was the wrong thing to do."

"Ostuda!" the fallen rider bellowed.

Geraint didn't hesitate. He turned and hurried around a tent displaying saddles and then sprinted awkwardly across the way to a narrow opening between two other tents.

Stopping only for a moment to get his bearings, before long he was a good distance away. He could hear the rider still shouting and Geraint decided that more distance was needed.

He looked up at the mountains, searching for the half dome that marked the southern end. Once he had it in his sights, he headed in that direction, staying as close to the tents as possible.

The sun sank lower. Geraint knew his family would be preparing the evening meal and would become concerned for him if he arrived too late.

He looked at the thoroughfare, but it was clogged with people, horses, and carriers. He would likely be trampled if he went back that way. Instead, Geraint made his way to the edge of the valley. His family was camped on the outskirts of the Tanaiste and taking this way would allow him to avoid the crowds and unwelcome attention.

While it was a long trek back, at least there were few people on this edge of the Tanaiste and Geraint felt safe enough to not to seek the protection of the shadows.

As he walked, Geraint wished he had thought of this route sooner. Nearly everyone was in the thick of the festival, so the going was far easier. The few people he did see were all servants. And, as they were mostly Duta'ut captives, they paid little attention to him. He wondered why he had not observed this before. Perhaps he would be better off with the Duta'ut after all.

A loud cheer rose from the camp. Someone must have done something especially daring. To the Dhervina, this was even better than winning a race.

Geraint wished he could be there. He missed the thrill of a close contest. At last summer's Kholedari festival, Yurki of his kereit had not only won an important race, he had bested kereit Borjigin by hanging from the stirrups to pick up an alaque and then returned to the saddle all while at full gallop.

Geraint examined the mountain slope beside him. Part of the hillside had a gentle slope that might allow him to climb higher. Maybe he would be able to see the races from there. Or even see the banners of kereit Jirgin.

Moving slowly so as not to stumble, Geraint made his way up the side of the mountain until he was overlooking the entire camp.

It was getting darker now. The sun cast long shadows as it sank behind the opposite mountain. The descending darkness made it difficult to see the colors on the other side of the valley.

But it was still light enough on this side and Geraint finally glimpsed the black and yellow banner further up the valley.

Clambering down, Geraint wondered why he hadn't felt the itch or heard the hum since that time on the cliff. Was it too far away? He scanned the great plain of the Tanaiste again. The Jirgin banners weren't much further away than they had been when he was on the cliff earlier.

What if the itch hadn't been caused by the Jirgin, after all? What if it was something else?

He wondered if Rhian had ever encountered something like the itch. He would ask her. It would be a good excuse to return and talk with her again. Maybe he could hear more of the dhavaras she had seen in the Duta'ut.

ANDRAS

As soon as the dhavara was gone, Andras darted forward and extended his hand to the Talfryn rider who was still floundering as he tried to regain his feet.

"Vinaka," the rider said as he brushed himself off clumsily, missing much of the dirt and straw.

"What did you do to the dhavara to make him cause you to lose your footing?" Andras asked.

"I did nothing," the rider said, nearly falling over again as he straightened indignantly.

"He likely took an insult where none was intended then," Andras said. "He is well known for that."

"It was but a short fall," the Talfryn rider said. "So perhaps he was not all that insulted."

"This time," Andras said. "I would watch for him in the final race. He has a wager on another rider and so may place a curse on you so that you lose."

"I did not know this of him," the Talfryn rider said. "I will be watchful. You have my thanks for your assistance this day."

Andras gave him a short nod of acknowledgment before walking away.

The dhavara was likely returning to his family's tent, so Andras sauntered back to his tent feeling much better than he had earlier.

Perhaps his luck had improved. He had no doubt the Talfryn rider would tell others and the whispers would grow. Enough complaints and the dheren would have no choice but to declare the dhavara ostraka.

GERAINT

The next day, Geraint again skirted the encampment on his way to find the black and yellow Jirgin banner. He had to stop frequently to rest and the sun was high and hot by the time he reached the middle of the valley. He stopped in the shade of a tent and took a few sips of water from his water skin.

Dust rose in giant clouds and from the sounds of the cheering, the races were well underway. Some of his apprehension ebbed away. Most of the warriors would be at the races, so perhaps he would be able to avoid trouble in the Jirgin camp, after all.

As the sun was high, there was little shade. So Geraint had no choice but to walk straight through the camp unconcealed. He stayed as close to the tents as possible to avoid being trampled by horses and drunken revelers. He also kept watch on possible escape routes in case of trouble. That was one way in which his size helped. There were so many places he could hide and escape detection.

After a couple of false turns, Geraint finally reached the tents flying the black and yellow banners. Unfortunately, he did not feel the itch or hear the humming.

That left him in a quandary. He had thought to follow the sound to the source and then go to the Guardian to ask what it meant. But no sound meant he was left without a way to discover the cause.

Maybe the sound had not come from the Jirgin, after all.

He knew he could not ask them if they knew what might be causing him to hear the humming. They would surely think him possessed and remove him from the Tanaiste immediately.

If that happened, he would never find the answers he was looking for.

He looked around uncertainly, but saw nothing that would give him a clue. He wandered past as many of the Jirgin tents as he could, but the itch didn't return.

Finally, Geraint decided to go see Rhian and see if she had any ideas.

He turned, thinking to go back to the edge of the encampment.

He froze. The fear that had seized him when Tegan and his friends chased him, returned.

Instead of the tents he had just passed, he was now looking at a wall of women.

Very large women.

And while their clothes were bright with festival finery, they were still dressed as if they were about to go into battle. Worse, the expressions on their faces were anything but festive.

"Greetings," Geraint said pleasantly, hoping his voice didn't shake.

"Why are you in our camp?" demanded a woman wearing an emblem of a curved black dagger on her vest.

Geraint realized that the truth would only make him look suspicious.

He gave them his best smile. "I heard the Great Khagan was camped near here and wanted to see for myself. But on the way I saw your banners. I have heard about the quality of your horses and wanted to see if it is true."

"And why would you want to know that?"

"I have a small talent as a breeder," Geraint said. "I had hoped to learn more from the Jirgin."

The woman's face darkened. "You want to place a curse on us so our horses will wither and die."

"No," Geraint protested. "I intend no ayna'al. I would never do that."

"He is just a boy," another woman said. "Perhaps he is truthful, this one."

"He is a dhavara. Everyone knows they bring nothing but ostuda. And he has the eyes of the sky. All know that means ayna'al." The first woman eyed him as if she would take his head right there.

"Maybe as adults," the second woman said. "But I have never heard of a child bringing misfortune. Perhaps a warning will be sufficient. After all, it is the Tanaiste and no one must be harmed."

Geraint watched nervously as the women looked at each other and then at him.

Finally, after what seemed like a lifetime, the first woman nodded.

"A warning then." The first woman fixed a black gaze on Geraint. "But know this, dhavara. Should you return, Tanaiste or no, we shall take you out beyond the valley."

Geraint knew that once outside the valley, they were no longer bound by the laws of the Tanaiste and he doubted they would simply send him on his way. Not with their reputation.

"Then I shall not return," Geraint said.

The women moved slightly, creating a narrow opening. Geraint wanted to hurry away, but forced himself to walk normally until he was completely clear of the Jirgin kereit.

Once he reached the edge of the encampment, he saw on a large rock until his legs stopped shaking.

The Tanaiste was turning out to be more perilous than he had expected. He hoped Rhian would know something.

Andras

Andras waited until the dhavara had been swallowed by the crowd before returning to the Jirgin camp.

The woman who had confronted the dhavara was shaking dirt from a saddle blanket while the others laughed at something. Andras walked over.

Their festival clothing was well worn and fraying in several places, branding them as minor Dhervina. That would give him the leverage he needed. They were more likely to listen to what he said and believe it than had they been of a major family. Better, they would talk with the others in their kereit.

"Why did you let him go?" he demanded.

The woman's black eyes glittered at him dangerously.

"And who are you to speak to me in that manner?" she asked unexpectedly. "You are but a child. Did your family teach you no manners?" She continued to shake the blanket, showering specks of debris all over him.

Andras swallowed his anger. She was much like his mother and he knew how to deal with women like that.

"I ask your forgiveness, Manari," he said, sounding as contrite as he knew how. "I have been so concerned about the presence of the dhavara at the Tanaiste this summer, I forgot myself."

As he expected, the old crone's face immediately softened. Better, she stopped shaking the blanket.

"Do you know something against this dhavara?" she asked.

"I do indeed," he said. "I had hoped that you did, as well, and were about to end the ostuda he brings on us all."

"What has he done?"

Out of the corner of his eyes, Andras saw the other women drawing closer.

"He has brought great misfortune on the kereits that accompany his on the Great Circle," he began. "Many horses have died. Children born, but who never live. Bad luck trading with the Duta'ut, even in places where once there was great good fortune. Even his sister has been driven to Khutulun out of fear."

This last was a gamble, but Andras knew it had been a good choice as the women began to murmur excitedly. Becoming Khutulun was sacred and only to be undertaken out of conviction. Not out of fear or an attempt to escape.

"Why has he been allowed to continue?" the woman demanded.

"The Dheren believe he should not be judged until he is of age. And now that he is of age, they do not see the misfortune he has caused. So they do nothing." Andras shrugged and spread his hands. "There is little I can do other than warn others. Which is why I had hoped you would stop him. Now he will put a curse on your tents."

"Why would he do that?" another woman asked. "He was not harmed."

"You frightened him. That has been sufficient in the past."

"What is your designation?" the first woman asked.

Andras supposed there was no getting out of that. "Andras of family Tuvas, kereit Malika, Kypchak Kishyn, Manari," he said.

"We thank you for your warning, Andras of Malika," she said formally. "We will think on what you have said."

Andras knew he could not push it any further. "Vinaka for your courtesy, Manari," he said. "My tent is at the south end of the valley should you wish to speak to me further."

He had bred the horse, now he would have to wait to see if it would yield a strong colt. Andras took his leave and returned to the southern end of the valley, satisfied that he had had the chance to flick the horse a little more. He would continue his watch on the dhavara. Perhaps he could find more that would rid him of the dhavara's presence for all time.

GERAINT

Geraint saw the banners of kereit Halaka with relief. At least here he did not have to hide his presence.

He stopped again near the tent of Manan Yorath. Once he was certain the family was not there, he peered inside.

The tent was empty.

"Rhian?"

There was no answer. Disappointed, he stepped outside the tent to return home. Then he saw her returning from the stream with two skins of water.

Rhian saw him a moment later and her face lit up with a huge smile.

Geraint smiled in return, happy to have made at least one friend at the Tanaiste.

Rhian placed the skins near the front opening of the tent.

"What brings you back?" Rhian asked as she poured the water into a large jar and covered it with a leather cap.

"I have a question you may be able to answer," Geraint said. "It is very strange and I do not know what it means."

She straightened and looked at him with a direct gaze.

"If I can," she said gravely.

He told her about the itch and the humming, all the while watching her face for any sign of revulsion, but Rhian's face simply looked thoughtful.

"You have been many places," Geraint said. "Perhaps you know something about what I experienced."

"I am not familiar with what you are describing," Rhian said after a time. "It is most unusual." She began arranging the pillows around the center carpets in preparation for the evening meal.

"I thought my visit to the Jirgin camp would help, but it did not," Geraint said. "And I don't know what to do next."

"There are few people with great learning among the Dhervina," Rhian said delicately. "Is your Guardian one of those people?"

"She is," he said. "But I had hoped you would know so I would not have to ask her. I do not want her to think I am possessed."

"She does cleansings, does she not?"

"She does."

"Perhaps there is something in your ears that you encountered on your journey here. It could be a simple matter to visit a healer."

"Possibly. I must think upon that." The difficulty would be in finding the lian to pay for the visit, but it did remove his concern of being thought possessed.

"That is all that comes to mind," Rhian said. "I could ask about it."

"Please don't ask questions," Geraint blurted out. "Most Dhervina already believe I am ostuda. Anything so strange will be considered proof of that."

"Then I will not," Rhian promised. "I will think on this question. Perhaps I can remember something that will help you."

"I would be honored, Rhian of Mentos," he said. "Perhaps we could enjoy the procession together at the end of the Tanaiste?"

"Perhaps," Rhian said. "I must ask if the family expects me to join them or if I can get permission to see it with someone else."

"Then I will stop by again to speak with you."

"I look forward to that Geraint of Halaka."

Without thinking, Geraint left by way of the front tent flap. To his dismay, three women were just outside the tent. They glared directly at him.

They made no move towards him and he walked away unaccosted. But as he went, he felt their hatred carve a hole in his back.

Tegan

Tegan cursed again as he left the races. His visit to the Khuvas camp had convinced him that their rider was the one to beat. But apparently no one had told the boy from kereit Alchi.

Kereit Khuvas was kin to the Talfryn and was likewise known for its fine riders. Their rider had defeated all comers easily.

Until the last race.

Tegan still could not believe how well the Alchi boy had ridden. But the Khuvas rider could still have won had it not been for the last jump. His horse had nicked the small tent while the Alchi horse had cleared it handily.

Ordinarily Tegan wouldn't have minded losing the five silver stallions. The race had been close and worthy of the Dhervina. What stuck in his throat was that the Alchi rider was barely of age. Worse, he was from the same kypchak as Tegan and their kereits often traveled together. How could he have missed seeing the boy race at the Makara or any of the other festivals this past summer?

Worse, the Alchi weren't known for *anything*. They weren't warriors or decent horse breeders or anything else worth mentioning. They tended goats and sheep and often didn't even attend the Tanaiste because their animals weren't allowed on the sacred grounds.

And while Tegan enjoyed a haunch of lamb as much as the next Dhervina, they weren't riders. They tended farkin sheep! So how had the boy learned to ride like that? And how had he managed to keep it such a secret that even Tegan had no idea?

Tegan still couldn't believe the boy had thrown a shirka straight up and then caught it while still in full gallop *and* beat the Khuvas rider to the finish line.

It was a worthy race, but Tegan had bet more than he should have and now he wouldn't be able to buy the new saddle he'd had his eye on.

Tegan scraped past a horde of revelers and jammed his foot into a tent peg he had overlooked.

The pain forced him to stop until the throbbing eased.

As he waited for the pain to ease, he caught sight of the dhavara waddling down the thoroughfare as if he belonged there.

In truth, Tegan had nearly forgotten the dhavara in the excitement of the races. He might not be able to get the new saddle he wanted, but he could certainly do something about the dhavara.

It was time someone did.

BRYS

Brys had never enjoyed the Tanaiste.

For her, it was seven sun cycles of oppressive heat. It was overcrowded and too dry compared to the southern plains where her kereit traveled. It had also been about duty without relief. For as long as she could remember, the long journey there, the work to set up and take down the tent and then the journey back to the south usually overshadowed all else in the seven sun cycles of the Tanaiste. Plus, there were always family obligations or work to be done that left little time for visiting or anything else, for that matter.

In a way, Brys hadn't minded that part. She had never enjoyed mindless chatter with other girls of her kereit. Nor had she wanted to indulge in idle speculation about the virility of the riders. That had never been of interest to her. But she had wanted to visit the Talfryn camp or the kereits of the other riders more often. She would have liked to wander the Tanaiste without also having to be concerned about her brother.

The best times had been when she had been able to steal away from the tent and talk to the riders or practice for the races. Then she had experienced a brief taste of freedom that made her yearn for more.

But now that she had made her pledge to the Khutulun, the Tanaiste felt like a different place.

Still getting used to the feel of the red Khutulun ribbons woven into her hair, she turned her head from side to side as if looking at the festival. But it was the way the red ribbons looked in her long black hair that caught her real attention.

They reminded her that she was now free from family obligations both present and future. Now she could live a life of *her* choosing. Now she could enjoy the finery and festivities.

She noticed an array of shirkas glittered in the sun as she made her way past a sheep roasting slowly over a great fire pit. She didn't have the lian to buy a slice, but she could look. And smell. Once she began her service with the Khutulun, she could earn several slices if she chose.

A display of huge half-moon shaped berdysz axes caught her eye. After seeing several at the Khutulun camp, she was eager to learn how to use one. Brys sidled over to get a closer look.

A rough voice cut into her thoughts.

"You cannot escape this time, dhavara!"

Brys' head whipped around, her ribbons and weapons forgotten. She ran towards the sound and cut through the gathering crowd.

"Got him!"

She burst through the crowd to see Geraint dangling from Tegan's fists, his legs kicking impotently.

The crowd suddenly quieted as Brys stopped mere feet away.

"Put him down now," she commanded. "You break the laws of the Tanaiste. Let him go!"

"He is ostuda," Tegan said.

Brys heard the uncertainty in his voice. Faint, but there. He had not expected to be challenged.

"He is under the protection of the Tanaiste. Let him down or the dheren will be called."

Tegan's head turned as he looked at the crowd, seeking support.

But the people who had once been so willing to watch a few moments earlier, now looked away.

"Now!" Brys' voice crackled through the noise of the festival like a whip.

Tegan released his hold, letting Geraint drop heavily to the ground.

Brys went over to her brother to make sure he hadn't been harmed, then faced Tegan.

"Let him be," she said. "The Tanaiste is no place for this."

His mouth twisted into a sneer. "You cannot protect him forever. When this Tanaiste is over, I will be ready. He is ostuda and has no place here."

"Only the dheren decide that," Brys said. "Not you."

"And will you always be at his side to make sure of that?" He looked her up and down contemptuously. "I think not. You will be with the Khutulun and then we can do what should have been done many summers ago."

He gave her another black look, then pushed his way through the crowd.

Even as Brys took Geraint's hand, the crowd dissipated, returning to their business.

"He is right, you know," Geraint said. "You cannot always be with me."

"I know."

They walked the rest of the way in silence.

RHIAN

Rhian hurried into the tent of supplies and quickly slipped a bit more dried food into the small basket she had secreted within another larger basket. She could only take a few moments here and there to avoid being caught and she lived in constant fear that Yorath would come looking for her and discover her cache.

The tent of supplies was her responsibility, so there wasn't much chance of the others coming upon her. Yorath, however, was another matter. He often searched her out here when he wanted the use of her body.

She moved quickly and had just returned to the main tent when Yorath, manan of Family Odegai, entered and Rhian sank to her knees and bowed her head as required.

"Up," he commanded. "I have heard disturbing news and would know the truth from you."

Startled, Rhian got to her feet, still keeping her gaze focused on the blue edging of the carpet beneath her feet.

"A neighbor told me you spoke to the dhavara," he accused. "Is this true?"

"I did," she said. "He asked the family name as he was honored at our presence among their Kypchak."

A blow sent her sprawling to the ground.

"You dare put our lives in the hands of a dhavara? You would bring ostuda upon our family?"

"No," Rhian protested. She pulled herself to her knees. "I would never do such a thing."

Another blow sent her sprawling yet again.

"You let him set foot in our tent?"

"Only for a moment," she said.

This time Rhian didn't have a chance to rise before a kick took all the air out of her. Rhian curled up on herself as she gasped for breath.

"You repay our hospital with treachery."

"No," she managed to gasp. "I did not know he was ostuda. Not until after. I would not have allowed it again. I swear by the Great Horse."

She cringed, expecting another blow, but there was only silence.

Finally she dared to look up. Yorath was glaring at her, but some of the rage had drained out of his eyes.

"I forget you do not know all our ways," he said finally. "Nevertheless, the law says that only blood payment by the person who invited the misfortune can erase the invitation. Should any ostuda befall our family this next summer, you will pay with your life."

Rhian struggled back to her knees despite the pain that made her light-headed and nauseous.

"I understand, Manan" she said.

"I will send the Guardian to conduct a cleansing. Do whatever she asks."

"As you command, Manan."

He took down the katra, the long vest, he wore only when he appeared before the Dheren or the Great Khagan. He glared at her as he adjusted it. Then he strode out.

Only then did Rhian allow herself to collapse into a more comfortable position so she could breath without pain. Her head hurt where he had struck her. She wondered if they had enough willow bark to ease the pain. She had not had a chance to add to the supply on the way to the Tanaiste.

Thank the gods he had not come upon her in the tent of supplies. He might well have knocked over the basket and discovered her secret. Then she thought about Geraint.

How could the Dhervina believe such a thing? Given the depth of hatred she had seen, it was astonishing he continued to live in their midst.

Rhian knew that Geraint was no more bad luck than anyone else. But after eight summers with the Dhervina, she knew how much superstition ruled their lives. It still surprised her because, in many ways, they were so much further advanced than the Duta'ut they encountered.

Rhian knew she had to warn Geraint somehow. He would most likely be killed if he showed up again. Tanaiste or not.

Then she thought of her own situation. She had been Yorath's prisoner long enough to know that he was serious when he said her life was forfeit. Anything could happen and usually did at the worst possible time. She didn't want to be blamed when that happened.

She would have to find a way to move her supplies out of the camp in case something went wrong and she had to leave sooner than she had intended.

YORATH

Aswirl in his katra manara, Yorath strode past tent and Dhervina alike, unseeing. His rage had subsided enough for him to manage himself as required at the Tanaiste. But anger still simmered as he made his way to the tent of the Dheren for kereit Malika.

The fools *had* to see that accepting the presence of a dhavara was inviting disaster.

Yorath had set his tent within Kypchak Kishyn only because of his daughter's pending alliance. Yet after only one sun cycle, his tent had been invaded by a dhavara who had undoubtedly left misfortune behind. Worse, the dhavara knew the family designation and could bring ostuda on them in the future.

Yorath had not considered the presence of a dhavara in Kypchak Kishyn when he agreed to the alliance with family Tuvas of kereit Malika. If the dhavara was a member of kereit Malika, then he would have to cancel the alliance even though it would cost him a considerable number of horses, gold, and other gifts.

And upset his daughter.

Yorath grimaced at the thought of the temper and tears she would undoubtedly unleash. It had been bad enough when he tried to make an alliance with another, more suitable family. But he could not allow his family to ally with any kereit containing a dhavara.

Yorath had to ask directions, but finally found the tent of the Dheren of kereit Malika. Fortunately, the flap was open when he arrived, indicating availability, and Yorath stepped inside.

The dim cool inside was a welcome respite from the heat and dust outside and Yorath let it soothe him while he waited.

The dheren sat on a cushion in front of the dheral, the carpet designating the law. A woman sat opposite.

While the carpets of the Dhervina were woven with many things, the dheral was woven only with horsehair from horses belonging to the Dhervina. It bore four colored stripes, one for each of the kypchaks and was always present during matters involving the law. Yorath had heard that each dheral was also charged by the great Crystal before going to a dheren. It was said that should any dheren not judge fairly and according to the way of the Dhervina, the carpet would turn black.

It had never happened as far as Yorath knew, but it was reassuring to know there were safeguards in place to keep the newer dheren in check.

Yorath stepped forward to leave room for other visitors, but not so close that he would have intruded on the proceedings with the woman.

Yorath noticed that this particular dheral was far from new, which gave him confidence. This dheren was no young fool. He would understand the way of the Dhervina and the importance of the ancient ways.

Yorath was glad of the wait as the dheren conducted the hearing with the woman. It allowed him to get his emotions under control and consider the best way to present the difficulty.

By the time the woman departed, Yorath was again in command of himself. He stepped forward slightly so the dheren could see him.

"Yorath of family Odegai, kereit Besut, Kypchak Olshyn."

"Welcome Manan Yorath of Besut. Please sit." The dheren indicated the hearing place before the dheral with a broad sweep of his hand.

Yorath stepped forward and sat cross-legged before the dheren.

"Will you partake of tea with me?" the dheren asked.

"I will."

Yorath wasn't so much agreeing to the tea as he was accepting the dheren's hospitality and judgment.

Yorath had heard younger men grumble about the practice. They wanted to get right to the point. But Yorath found great comfort in the ritual. It established formality and the serious nature of the proceedings. This was not an ordinary conversation and Yorath didn't want it treated as such.

The dheren poured the dark tea and handed the cup to Yorath. He then poured a cup for himself. A plate of sweet dates was placed on the carpet. Yorath ate one of the dates and then drank the bitter tea. The dates represented the sweetness of justice, while the tea represented the bitterness of life.

Yorath had heard it said that there was a truth serum in the tea to ensure honest dealing. He rather doubted the story, but approved of the idea.

"I come seeking enlightenment," Yorath said.

"May you find enlightenment here," the dheren said.

Both men now finished the tea.

When he was finished, Yorath put the cup back on the plain wooden tray and waited for the dheren's next words.

"So what brings you to my tent this day?" the dheren asked.

"I was finalizing an alliance for my daughter with family Tuvas of kereit Malika. However, I had forgotten there is a dhavara who is made welcome in Kypchak Kishyn. This concerns me greatly. Especially as the dhavara visited my tent earlier today and obtained my designation."

The dheren nodded. "I am familiar with the dhavara. You can rest assured that he does not belong to kereit Malika. He is of kereit Halaka and so the ostuda of his family will not taint your family's line."

"Ahhh. That is very good to hear," Yorath said.

"As to his visit to your tent, I understand that the boy in question has only come of age this summer. Your tent has excited a great deal of curiosity. I believe that simple curiosity was to blame for his presence at your tent."

"He entered my tent," Yorath said, raising his voice before he could stop himself. "Apologies, dheren. I was quite dismayed when I discovered the trespass and let my feelings get the best of me."

"I understand. The boy, however, has a mere thirteen summers and is unlikely to have brought ostuda into your tent as yet. I know the Guardian for Kypchak Kishyn will be only to happy to perform a cleansing for you to make sure there is no possible ostuda attached to your tent."

"Is the boy to be named Dhervina, then?"

"The boy has shown no indication to trouble," the dheren said carefully. "There have been no reports of misfortune in all the summers he has been with Kypchak Kishyn."

"But now he is of age," Yorath pressed. "Now is when he will be dangerous."

The dheren took a deep breath and closed his eyes.

Yorath waited patiently. By the accoutrements in the tent, Yorath knew this dheren kept to the old ways. But he also knew that individual dheren answered to the Great Council of Dheren and could not always act according to their understanding and beliefs.

Finally the dheren opened his eyes.

"As yet there is no determination. We are relying on those Dhervina who know anything to the detriment of the dhavara to come forward. So far no one has seen him doing anything untoward. Do you have something to report?"

Yorath shook his head. "No. He merely came to my tent. It was unwelcome, but so far as I know he did nothing but ask a question."

It pained him to make the admission, but he knew that to do otherwise, especially during the Tanaiste, would be ruin and even worse misfortune than the dhavara could ever bring.

"Unless there is trouble, there is nothing more I can tell you with regard to the dhavara. Therefore, the matter is concluded," the dheren said. "Is there anything else for which you look for enlightenment?"

"No. I thank you for your wisdom. I have brought a small gift that I hope you will find acceptable."

He drew out three gold stallions and placed them on the dheral. Yorath knew that one lian was the usual offering, but the larger amount would encourage the dheren to assist him further in the future.

The dheren nodded his approval. "That is most satisfactory."

Yorath unfolded his legs and stood. He bowed once to the dheren and left the confines of the tent.

When he stepped outside, the blazing heat and undimmed sun made his head hurt. He wanted nothing more than to return to the cool of his tent, but he still needed to find the Guardian to do a cleansing before he would feel comfortable stepping inside his tent again.

Fortunately, the Guardian was not otherwise engaged. After he explained the difficulty, she followed Yorath back to his tent and Yorath waited outside while the Guardian entered and performed the cleansing ritual.

When she finally emerged, Yorath handed the Guardian three gold stallions for her services.

Guardian Seren nodded in acknowledgment and placed them in a small pouch at her waist.

"I felt a good deal of anger within, Manan Yorath," the Guardian said. "I have cleansed that. I did not detect any ostuda or curse, so I believe you to be safe. To be sure, I placed a deflection spell on your tent that will ward off any attempt by the dhavara to cause you ostuda in the future."

"I thank you for your service, Guardian Seren," Yorath said. "It has brought my mind immeasurable peace."

"I am pleased to be of use," Guardian Seren said. "Do you wish me to speak to the boy?"

"I had thought to speak to his family myself," Yorath admitted.

If you would like me to join you, I will be only to happy to do so," she said. "Perhaps I can tell you if the dhavara is a danger or not."

Yorath knew the Guardians had abilities beyond that of the ordinary Dhervina, but had not expected this.

He would have preferred to go on his own and unleash his anger in such a way that the cursed dhavara would never dare come within a gallop of his tent again. But using the Guardian might be more useful.

"I would be honored," he said.

"Unleashing anger often only causes more trouble and brings on misfortune," she added. "Find me when you are ready to visit."

"Would after the evening meal suit?" Yorath asked.

"I will be ready." And then she was gone in a whirlwind of white and black.

SEREN

Seren returned directly to her tent after leaving Yorath. She would normally have visited with others, but she was disturbed by what she had sensed while in Manan Yorath's tent.

She had told him truly that she had picked up his anger. She had not mentioned his slave's fear and pain as it would only have embarrassed him. She also had not told him of the healing she had performed on the slave.

Under other circumstances she would have warned him that violence was not permitted at the Tanaiste. But she had felt the undercurrent of anger still running through him and knew that her words would only increase his anger. The thread was clear that his anger could easily burst forth and cause even more damage.

What had disturbed her most, though, was the same faint trace of energy she had felt on the first day of the Tanaiste when the crystal had activated itself so unexpectedly.

Even though the energy was faint, it was undeniably there. If she had experienced it on her own, she might have doubted herself. But she had brought the large crystal to the healing and that had heightened her sensitivity.

There was no mistake.

But who had left that trace?

It wasn't the slave. Seren had seen that immediately. It could possibly be Yorath's daughter, but she doubted that, as well. The signature was too weak. If it was the daughter, the energy would have been much stronger.

She would have to move with caution. Yorath belonged to a different kypchak. If there was a crystal Talent in his family, she would have to inform the Guardian for the Ulshyn Kypchak.

Seren closed her tent flap and placed the box in the place of honor.

Instead of removing her official robes, she commanded silence and opened the lid of the box.

Seren took the large white crystal out and held it in both hands.

Taking a deep breath, she closed her eyes and sent her mind out.

But no matter where she looked, she was unable to feel the energy thread she was looking for.

Seren finally returned to her body and placed the crystal in the box. Exhausted by her efforts, she removed her robes and stepped into the ritual bath that would cleanse her and renew her.

Afterwards, she lay on her sleeping mat to recover before Manan Yorath returned. Instead of falling into sleep as she had expected, her mind raced as she considered the implications of the energy she had felt in Yorath's tent.

Was it possible the dhavara was the crystal Talent?

If so, what did that mean for the Dhervina?

TEGAN

Tegan waited only until the girl was three tents away before he began following her.

Kelmon grabbed his arm. "Where are you going?"

"I want to know where their tent is."

"What do you intend?"

Tegan grinned. "We could be rid of that dhavara before the moon hides behind Khurtagin." The mountain peak was the highest and tethered the western end of the valley, so the moon was hidden from sight early in the evening. "But first we need to see where their tent is."

Tegan made sure to hang back enough so the dhavara and his sister wouldn't see them, but the girl must have felt secure in the Tanaiste and never looked back.

Finally, the two entered a tent off to the side of their kereit with nothing but the mountain slope next to it.

It would be a simple matter to do what he had in mind once it became dark enough, Tegan thought.

He tugged on Kelmon's vest and gestured him off to the side. "Look how close they are to the pass." He pointed at the southern entry to the Tanaiste which was only a few gallops beyond the one belonging to the dhavara. They would have to pass by three other kereits, but that should be a simple matter if they waited until the time of darkness.

"What are you thinking to do?"

Tegan looked around carefully. There were too many Dhervina nearby, so he pulled Kelmon further away.

"It would be an easy matter to drag their tent into the pass," he said.

"Where they would no longer be in the valley," Kelmon finished with a slow grin.

Tegan nodded. "Then we could be rid of them with no insult to the Tanaiste."

"But why not wait until the Council of Dheren have made their decision? They may decide to ban him. Then he will be gone with no trouble on our part."

"And if they decide he should be Dhervina? Then what?"

"We deal with him then," Kelmon said. "It will be the end of the Tanaiste and less chance of trouble for us."

Tegan could see the sense of that, but he wanted to do something *now*. Then his gaze was caught by the sight of a boy across the way. He elbowed Kelmon and tilted his head in the boy's direction.

"Who is that?" Kelmon asked.

"I don't know," Tegan said. "But he doesn't look any happier about the dhavara than we are. And his tent is close. He might be of some use to us."

Tegan made his way across to where the boy was standing, leaving Kelmon to follow. But as he got closer, the boy's eyes suddenly widened in shock. The next moment he had ducked into the tent behind him like a rabbit ducking for cover.

Tegan stopped at the open tent flap.

"Hey, boy!" he called. "I want a word with you."

He heard a whisper from inside and then a woman came out and blocked the entrance. She was solidly built and dressed in festival finery that spoke of wealth. She looked Tegan up and down slowly and then did the same with Kelmon, her gaze bold and contemptuous.

Tegan clenched his fists in frustration. If it weren't for the Tanaiste, he would have not hesitated to put the woman in her place. As it was, he would have to be careful if he wanted assistance from the boy.

Then recognition kicked in.

"Manari," he said as respectfully as he could. "I had hoped to have a word with your son."

"You and your friend can take yourselves back to whatever house you dragged here," she told him, the insult clear. Only the Duta'ut made their homes in a wooden structure.

"But..."

She cut him off. "The last time you had a "word" with my son, he had bruises for a full moon cycle. He is to be allied with Kypchak Ulshyn this day and will have no dealings with the likes of either of you."

"But I only...." he began again, then thought better of it as he saw the fierce light in her eyes.

"I cry your pardon, Manari," he said, tapping the center of his forehead in respect. "I had but a question for your son, but I will ask someone else."

"This is the Tanaiste," she said. "And many still believe in the old ways. So when you ask someone a question, remember that many are watching."

Tegan clenched his teeth to control his anger and merely dipped his head in acknowledgment and turned away.

Once they were a good distance away, he turned his head and spat, sending up a small puff of dust.

"Haiduc," he muttered.

Kelmon's head whipped around to see if anyone was close enough to hear. "Be careful," he hissed and put his hand on Tegan's arm. "Her family is very powerful."

Tegan knocked Kelmon's hand away. "She dared to speak to me as if I was a Duta'ut."

"You did drag the boy behind your horse for a good distance during the last Makara festival."

"Too bad I didn't run his head into one of the boulders along the river," Tegan said through clenched teeth. "Would have taught them a little more respect."

"He's still a boy," Kelmon said. "He wasn't likely going to be of much use, in any event."

Tegan looked back at the tent. He didn't say anything, but if he got the chance, he would repay their insults right after he finished with the dhavara.

"It's that farkin dhavara," he said, understanding dawning.

"What?" Kelmon drew back as he stared at him.

"Dhavaras bring nothing but ostuda," Tegan said. "All Dhervina know this to be true. This simply proves it. I have had nothing but ostuda since this Tanaiste began. It *must* be his doing."

Kelmon nodded slowly. "We should report this to the dheren. That will help them in their decision."

Tegan spat again. "May ostuda fall on their heads. They will do nothing."

"Perhaps not," Kelmon said, his hands spread to show he had no part in their decision. "But if we tell them of the trouble he has caused, they have to listen. If they do not have him banned, then we can step in. Then there will be few who will not join us. There is plenty of time."

Tegan could see the wisdom of his friend's words. "It would also allow us to get the others to help if needed."

Kelmon nodded. "Let's find Jolan and the others and we can make plans. They are probably still at the races."

Tegan looked back at the dhavara's tent, marking it for later before following Kelmon back towards the center of the Tanaiste.

GERAINT

It wasn't until they were back in their tent that Geraint noticed the red ribbons. Even though it was dim inside, the ribbons bounced and shone as Brys crossed the tent.

Geraint stopped at the water jug and poured water into two cups, handing one to his sister.

"When did you decide to become Khutulun?" he asked.

"Three summers ago," she said. "You remember the Khutulun who rode with our kereit on the Great Circle when we were having so much trouble with the Duta'ut along the river Tywin? They guarded our horses and protected us. I knew then that I was meant to be one of them."

"So you never wanted an alliance."

She shook her head, setting the ribbons dancing again. "Never."

Now a great deal made sense to Geraint. Brys had evaded his questions, so he had known something was on her mind. But he had never guessed it was this.

"Does Andras know?"

She looked at him sideways, eyes sharp with suspicion.

"Yes. Why?"

"He is always mooning over you," Geraint shrugged. "And he has been following me. Perhaps he thought he could find you by following me."

Brys shook her head. "Unlikely. I spoke with him when we arrived. He knows I am to be Khutulun."

She really looked at him then and Geraint felt as if she had suddenly acquired the ability to see deep into his kha.

"He is following you in the hopes of catching you doing something that will get you banned," she said flatly. "He has made no secret of his hatred of you. This is his last chance to do something about it."

"Would he do that?" Geraint blurted out, shocked. He couldn't imagine hating someone that much.

"Of course," Brys said. "So you must be very cautious. There are only four sun cycles more and then you will be safe."

"I wonder," Geraint said and then told her about his encounter with the Jirgin earlier.

"I am coming to believe I will never be safe as long as I am with the Dhervina," he said finally.

"You will be leaving then?"

Geraint's surprise must have written itself all over his face.

"You spoke of it when we first arrived," she said. "So you must have been thinking about it for some time."

He nodded. "I spoke to a slave from Kypchak Ulyshyn. She told me that there are many dhavara among the Duta'ut. I could find a place there."

"That is good," Brys said. "Then I wouldn't have to worry about you. I will not be able to protect you once the Tanaiste is over."

He grinned. "Have I been that difficult?"

"Sometimes," she laughed. "But what if the dheren confirm you as full Dhervina?"

He thought about it. "Is that likely to change anything? I will still be a dhavara and there are many who will never accept me. No matter what the dheren decide." He finished the last of the water in a gulp. "I can't run fast and I don't want to have to hide all the time."

"So you are decided?"

"I don't know."

"What did you think to do if you left?"

All the dreams and ideas he had had before arriving at the Tanaiste came trickling back and suddenly the idea of leaving the Dhervina didn't seem so daunting.

"I thought perhaps to find work with the horses of the Duta'ut. The last time we visited Tranynt and Penrhyd, they seemed to need someone good with horses. I could start there."

Brys nodded. "That could work. I remember Penrhyd in particular. They have always been friendly and have said several times that they were most pleased with our father's skill with their horses. You could stay with the kervan until you reach there."

He nodded. "That would take several moon cycles and give me time to prepare."

Brys looked away suddenly.

Geraint waited a suitable length of silence before speaking again. "Are you feeling quite well?"

"This talk reminds me that I have my own goodbye's to say. It is harder than I had expected," she said. "All that is familiar will now be gone."

Geraint nodded. "Nothing will be the same after this Tanaiste."

"No."

"Do you want to return your ribbons?"

She looked around the tent as if the answers might be lurking in the shadows, then shook her head. "No. But I must leave all this behind. It is everything I have known. I want to do this, but I thought it would be easier."

"Our parents will still be here," he reminded her. "You can visit them next summer. And when you go on the Great Circle as a Khutulun, you could visit me at Penrhyd."

"Yes, but it will no longer be my home."

"I will be leaving, so it could be, if you want."

Brys smiled. "No. I would be Khutulun even if you were not a dhavara. It is not your doing."

Geraint felt a surge of gratitude. Now he did not have to feel as if he had destroyed her life.

"What about Andras?" he asked.

"Ignore him," Brys advised. "There is little he can do now. If you remain cautious, at the end of the Tanaiste he will be unable to harm you."

SEREN

"No, that one." Seren pointed at the tunic, long pants, and long vest she usually wore only at her most important ceremonies.

"The katra manara, Guardian?" her handmaid asked even while taking the garments off their peg.

Seren had not often seen Pryderi taken by surprise.

"I want Manan Yorath to see the weight of the Guardians so he understands the import of his actions and beliefs," Seren said as she began donning the black pants and tunic. "Then he will know I do not consider this matter to be trivial. I want him to think on what he says and does. Especially at the Tanaiste."

Pryderi nodded her understanding and helped Seren into the massive over vest. The vest was pure white with crystals embroidered into it so that it sparkled when she walked. Black and white ribbons were woven into her hair and the ends trailed down nearly to her waist.

Unlike the rest of the Dhervina, she did not weave bells into her hair. When she walked, it was in complete silence.

And tonight she would have the Great Crystal with her.

She had originally thought to dress plainly and wear only the small crystal that nestled in the base of her throat. But the hint of Talent she had felt at Yorath's tent earlier had altered the importance of this visit.

Going to the place of honor, Seren picked up the box containing the crystal of Kypchak Kishyn with both hands. She would not carry it herself for this visit. She wanted it close, but not obvious.

The crystals on her vest would magnify the energy and would make it seem as if her power resided more in her person than it did in the crystal. The perception of power went a long way to dealing with the common Dhervina who could be stubborn and unruly at the best of times.

She would have Pryderi carry the large crystal for this visit. It would also be useful to have her impression of the visit even though Pryderi did not have the deep Ability required of a Guardian. On occasion her handmaiden was able to pick up things Seren might miss in the swirl of emotion.

Pryderi had come to her as a young girl and had initially shown some promise as a crystal Talent. But the gift had never grown and, unable to command the crystal, she was only able to assist Seren. The ability to harness the power of crystal was rare, so the assistance of women like Pryderi and Owena who had some talent was crucial. Without assistants, the work of the Guardians would be taxing beyond measure.

Once everything was prepared, her other handmaid, Owena, joined her. They stood one on each side of the tent opening and opened the flap, revealing Manan Yorath waiting just beyond in the swirling dust and remains of the heat. The sun had descended behind Khurtagin and most of the valley now lay in shadow. The earlier shouts and cheers for the racers had quieted to murmurs from people tired from sun and heat as they returned for the evening meal.

Seren loved this time of day. A blue haze lay over the valley as the strength of the sun retreated and the cool of the evening began chasing away the heat.

It was at moments like this that she could feel the truth that the Tanaiste was indeed the place at the top of the world. The feeling filled her and humbled her. Behind her, the crystal of Kypchak Kishyn vibrated, its energy reaching well beyond the box.

Seren followed Manan Yorath to the tent of the dhavara. She had sent a servant earlier to find the tent and prepare the family for her visit as she knew Yorath would not. She suspected he would have preferred to catch them unprepared and so have an advantage due to their embarrassment.

When she arrived at the tent, she was pleased to see all correct preparations had been made and the family was standing outside to greet them. Behind her, she could feel Yorath's displeasure and she smiled to herself. She did not like it when the wealthy or powerful sought to demean the ordinary Dhervina.

While clearly not wealthy, the family she saw before her, like all Dhervina, were proud and neat. They were clothed in festival finery that had clearly been recently brushed free of dust. The ground in front of the tent had also been raked clean of dust and weeds.

Seren felt the crystals on her vest begin vibrating with an intensity unlike any she had ever before encountered.

She looked at the four people before her and noticed the dhavara was wincing slightly. If he was the one setting off the crystal, the pain had to be intense, so it said a lot for the boy that a small wince was the only evidence of his discomfort.

The crowd that had gathered began murmuring and Seren looked down, only then realizing the crystals on her vest were glowing.

So much power.

She looked at the girl, hoping she was the one, but it clearly was not her. Her gaze went back to the boy. She had come half expecting the boy might have the Talent, but the power was unexpected. Seren wished she could explore this further, but it would have to wait until the current matter was dealt with.

"We make you welcome, Guardian. It is an honor to have you visit our miserable tent," the father said.

"It is my honor that you allow me to visit you," she returned.

"Would you care to enter and share a cup of tea with us?"

"I would be my good fortune to do so," she said.

The formalities satisfied, Geraint's father led the way into the tent.

Seren and Pryderi followed, but Yorath remained well outside any possible influence or contamination.

Inside the tent, Seren stood in the center facing the family members who arranged themselves in a semi circle before her. Pryderi would remain standing behind her until the visit was concluded. The ceremonial mat looked as if it had seen little use, but it was correctly placed and beautifully woven. The border was the rich green of their kypchak with the family emblem of the crescent moon done in the deep yellow of their kereit in the center.

The crystals began vibrating again and she looked at each member of the family in turn closely.

Her gaze returned to the dhavara. He was hiding it well, but she could tell he was hearing the crystal.

How is this possible?

Seren then sat cross-legged upon the visitor's pillows. The family followed suit.

The woman poured the tea and the girl carried a cup over to Seren. The girl's red Khutulun ribbons contrasted beautifully against her long black hair. There were no bells with her ribbons, which meant she had made her pledge, but had not yet been initiated. She was tall and Seren could see her strength. Seren felt no resonance and knew the girl had no crystal Talent.

A shame. Her energy was strong and clear, but she would be an asset to the Khutulun.

Seren accepted the tea and drank with the others. The girl knelt next to Seren in order to take the cup.

Seren placed a finger on the girl's arm. "You have made a good decision."

Then she felt a coldness and stopped. She did not like what she felt, but the image was not clear.

"Vinaka, Guardian." The girl dipped her head in thanks and returned the cup to the ceremonial mat.

Seren returned her attention to the dhavara.

"I understand you are Geraint of family Tumen, kereit Halaka, Kypchak Kishyn."

Geraint sat up straighter. "I am."

"Manan Yorath has told me you went to his tent earlier."

She could tell that he was surprised. He must have thought this visit had some other purpose.

"I did."

"What did you do there?"

"I asked the servant whose tent it was. I wanted to know if it was true there was going to be an alliance with our kereit. It was very exciting."

"I'm sure it was."

Seren opened her mind to the boy. There was definitely something there. She just didn't know what it was. The crystal around her neck was quiet now, but she had not mistaken the force with which it had vibrated earlier. If he was in the earliest stages of his Ability, then it would make sense that it came and went.

"Did he do something wrong?" the father asked finally, apparently unable to bear the silence.

Seren brought her attention back to the task at hand.

"I feel no malice from the boy and I do not believe he did anything wrong. The difficulty is that Manan Yorath is a superstitious man and prefers not to have a dhavara step inside his tent." Seren saw no need to mask the truth.

The light faded from Geraint's eyes and he suddenly seemed smaller. "I understand."

"There are many superstitious Dhervina who will see ayna'al in everything you do. It does not make you ayna'al or ostuda. But it does present a difficulty."

She could tell the boy was prepared for the worst in the way he squared his shoulders.

"I ask that you not enter any tent unless the family has invited you. That way, you will avoid the upset an accidental trespass might cause. Please especially do not enter Manan Yorath's tent as he has said that you are unwelcome there."

Geraint nodded his understanding.

"It is unfair to ask this of you, but my hope is that this will keep you safe. You will undoubtedly need to be careful. Even after you are confirmed as a full Dhervina."

"Do you truly think they will allow me to be Dhervina?" he asked. His voice made it clear he thought it unlikely.

"I do. There is no reason why you should not be. I caution you, though, that even once you are deemed Dhervina, there are many who will not be willing to accept you."

"I know."

"I also ask that you come to visit me in my tent after the morning meal," Seren told him now. "There is another matter on which I would examine you."

"What is it?" His face reflected concern.

His anxiety should have caused the crystal to activate, even slightly, but nothing happened.

"This is not the place. I will tell you when we see each other next."

She reached out her hand and the girl came over and helped Seren rise.

Seren turned her attention to the entire family. "Vinaka for your hospitality this evening Family Tumen of kereit Halaka, Kypchak Kishyn."

She bowed to the family, then turned towards the tent opening. Geraint and his sister opened the flap for her and bowed as she passed.

Seren felt a brief flare of something as she passed the boy, but it was gone nearly as fast as it had appeared. Summers of training kept her pace steady as she returned to the open air where the evening had already lost the heat of the day.

Yorath was waiting and Seren stopped to speak to him.

"I have examined all of them. There is no shadow of ill intent or misfortune. The boy has also agreed to never enter your tent without permission."

"Which will never be given."

"He understands that," Seren said. "You should have no lingering fear or concern for your family."

He bowed. "Again, your kindness and assistance are most appreciated, Guardian. May you have a blessed Tanaiste."

He bowed once again, handed her two more gold stallions and then strode away, vanishing into the maze of tents.

Seren returned to her tent, both troubled and elated.

Pryderi returned the crystal to the Place of Honor, then returned to assist Owena in removing the vest.

"What did you experience?" Seren asked Pryderi as her handmaidens freed her from the weight of the vest.

"I saw the crystals on the katra manara glow when we arrived at the dhavara's tent," Pryderi answered. "I felt a slight vibration, but do not know if it was from the crystal or those of your vest."

"Did you sense the presence of another Talent during our visit?"

The two handmaidens looked at each other in surprise, then Pryderi shook her head. "No, Guardian."

"I have invited the boy here after our morning meal tomorrow," she told them.

"The dhavara?" Owena put out her hand, palm out and two fingers forked, as if to ward off ayna'al.

"The boy is not ayna'al simply because he is a dhavara. He may have a rare Talent and I need to examine him."

"The dhavara?" Pryderi asked in surprise.

"Indeed."

"As you wish, Guardian," Owena said, but her face spoke other thoughts.

"Do you want to work with the crystal this night?" Pryderi asked.

Seren shook her head. "There is much I need to learn, but I have been severely depleted by the events of this day," she said.

"I will work with the crystal in the morning. Perhaps I will find the answers I seek then. If the boy has Talent, I will have to consider what that may mean for us, as well as for the Dhervina."

"But how can a boy have Talent?" Owena asked.

"It may be that his Talent is not for crystal even though his presence causes the crystal to respond to him," Seren said.

While a part of her hoped that the boy's Talent belonged elsewhere, another desperately hoped that his was a rare kind of crystal Talent. Then she would be the one to teach him and guide him in the direction she chose.

"But what if his Talent is for crystal," Pryderi asked. "Would that not mean the fulfillment of the prophesy?"

"According to one tradition," Seren conceded. "But another puts it in the hands of a woman. There have been many discussions among the Guardians about the chosen one, but none has been able to decide which is correct."

"It could not be a dhavara," Owena said firmly. "The Great Horse would never permit that."

Seren smiled. "One never knows for certain what the Great Horse will choose," she said. "It could even be that the Great Horse has no control over the one to fulfill the prophesy."

"Not... not have control?" Owena stopped in her place, water sloshing onto the carpets.

"Watch what you are doing, Owena," Seren said sharply. "Water is not to be wasted. We are not the Duta'ut who have many rivers."

"Pardon, Guardian." Owena poured the remainder of the water into the tub she had been filling.

"It may not matter to the Great Horse who fulfills the prophesy," Seren said. "Or it could be that the prophesy is older even than the Great Horse." She shrugged and spread her hands. "All we can do is what we were trained to do. It may be the boy and it may not. Either way, we will discover that for ourselves."

With that, Seren let Pryderi remove the last of her clothing and she slipped into the tub of hot water.

As her two handmaidens went to prepare the evening meal, Seren thought of how it would be if the boy was the Khevira of the prophesy. And the change it would bring for her. Instead of being the Guardian of the least respected kypchak of the Dhervina, she would be the most honored.

If the boy was the Khevira, it would be many summers before he was ready to meet the challenge. And there were likely many summers after that before his talent with the crystal was needed.

But the hint of fire and ash she had felt spoke of something very near and very soon. Then, as if a chill wind blew through the tent, she remembered the faint thread of something cold she had felt when she had touched the girl's arm earlier.

Whatever death that feeling bespoke, it would likely occur after the Tanaiste, but it was strong enough that Seren knew it would happen soon.

And somehow the girl was in the middle of it.

BRYS

As soon as the evening meal was over, Geraint gestured to her and Brys followed him outside.

"Would you be willing to do me one last kindness?" he asked once they were clear of the tent.

"If I can," Brys said, momentarily glad she would be joining the Khutulun after the midday meal tomorrow. She regretted the thought almost immediately. It was not his fault he was a dhavara and he seldom asked for anything.

"Would you be willing to take a message for me?"

She looked at him with surprise. "Who is it you cannot speak with yourself?"

"A servant in the tent of Manan Yorath," he said. "I spoke with her and promised I would return to speak with her again. She told me she has seen other dhavara among the Duta'ut. I thought to ask her more. If there are already some, why not one more? But I do not want to cause her trouble."

"Why do you need to tell her you will not return?" For Brys it was an easy matter. "The woman is a slave."

"She is my friend," Geraint said. "She was trying to help me."

"Then I also owe her a debt of gratitude," Brys said. "I will do as you ask."

"She is easy to find," Geraint said. "Her name is Rhian and she has hair the color of fire. I have seen her fetching water after the morning meal."

It was little enough to ask, Brys thought. Especially since he could not go in person. It would also be good to see what kind of woman this Rhian was. As a slave, she was likely to resent the Dhervina. Brys wanted to make sure this woman had no ayna'al intent towards her brother. This Tanaiste was already dangerous enough as it was.

GERAINT

That night Geraint dreamed of fire and an all consuming anger. He woke with a start, shouts and the feel of fire searing his skin still filling his mind.

The light of the sun had not yet entered this end of the valley and the rest of his family was still asleep. Outside, he heard only the occasional nicker from the horses. The hubbub that permeated the air during the day had not yet started and the quiet soothed Geraint's jagged emotions.

He still didn't know what to do. His plan to leave the Dhervina had been shaken by the Guardian's words telling him that he would be granted full membership after all. More, the request to come to her tent suggested she knew he had had a reaction to something during her visit.

Still, there were too many like Yorath or Tegan who would not accept him no matter what the Council of Dheren or the Guardian decided.

But the idea that he might be able to stay pulled at him. The Duta'ut could be unpredictable and the path outside the Dhervina would be difficult. If he stayed, he could be with people he knew in the family tent. While they were not wealthy, he would not trade their tent for any of those with horses beyond counting.

His mother was known for the excellence of her weaving and her rugs had made the tent more than comfortable. While she sold or bartered the rugs she made, she kept the best for the family tent. One of Geraint's favorites was the one under her sleeping mat. It had a brilliant red and blue border that she said reminded her of a kervan she'd encountered when still a girl. She often talked about the way it came through a mirage out of the east and was laden with colors and goods she had never seen since.

Many of the things she had seen in that kervan were woven into her rugs. This one had a huge bird in red, gold, green and blue in the center.

Near the tent flap, his father's bow lay ready for the hunt even though they would not hunt during the Tanaiste. His father kept it there so it would always be ready. Geraint was proud of his father's ability with the bow. Had he not been born so small and deformed, the bow would have passed to him on his father's death.

If he left, what would happen to the bow? It wasn't as if Geraint would ever be able to use it. But it would have been a comfort to him once his father went on to ride with the Great Horse.

As he sat on his mat in the grey dawn, Geraint decided to wait and see what happened. He could always leave. But it didn't have to be now.

Maybe things would get better once he was confirmed as full Dhervina.

Seren

When Seren awoke, the energy of the people outside pressed in on her like a score of horses standing on her chest. Her head throbbed and the memory of dreams filled with fire and ash had left a taste of death in her mouth. Although it was still not yet light, Seren knew she would be unable to sleep any longer and she hit a small bell with a mallet to summon Pryderi.

Working with the crystal could be difficult even in the best of circumstances, but it was nearly impossible when every part of her body felt as if it had been beaten with stones.

A dose of willow bark and a cloth dipped in cold water finally reduced the pain to a less troublesome level. Now she could use the crystal to remove what remained.

The small crystal around her neck, Seren walked over to the box holding the sacred crystal of the kypchak. Holding the crystal in both hands as required, she sat cross-legged on a large cushion.

As she had been trained, Seren began by opening her mind to the crystal. The key to the morning ritual was to think about nothing, not even ask a question. Just open her mind as if it was empty sky and let the power of the crystal move into her.

On most occasions she looked forward to the ritual at sun rise. There seemed to be more clarity and fewer conflicting energies in the early time before the sun rose over the mountains.

But not today.

Today she could still feel the remnants of the previous day. As her mind slid into the crystal, she again experienced a faint, unsettling undercurrent running darkly through like a black snake. When she reached for it to see if she could see it more clearly, it vanished as if made of ash. Time and again it slithered just beyond her grasp until Seren finally ended the ritual feeling unsatisfied.

"You are still unsettled," Pryderi said as she helped Seren to her feet.

Seren nodded. "Something is wrong, but it disappears into smoke when I get too near." She closed the lid on the crystal.

It was the first time she had had any difficulty reading the crystal and a line from the prophesy came to mind.

"There will come a time of great destruction," Seren whispered.

"Guardian?" Pryderi stared at her.

"The prophecy," Seren said. "It is much on my mind this summer."

She looked at Pryderi and then away. There was nothing more to be said. If the prophesy was beginning to manifest at long last, there was little she or anyone could do.

By the time the dhavara arrived, Seren had managed to gather her mind into a semblance of calm. She dressed in plain white pants and tunic with a plain black over vest. She wove white ribbon in her hair and hung the small crystal around her neck on a silver chain.

When Pryderi announced the boy, Seren opened the lid on the box. Only then did she step to the side to face the opening.

"Let him enter." But her eyes were on the crystal, not the dhavara as he approached.

As she suspected, the crystal began to glow. The boy stopped and put his hands to his ears.

Seren waited to see what he would do.

The boy began to hum. As he hummed, he removed his hands from his ears and stared at the crystal.

The crystal glowed even brighter.

Seren tried to link her mind with his, but it was as if there was a wall of granite blocking her way.

She had never before had difficulty linking with another mind. Especially that of a child. That this boy was able to block her with no training told her much of the ability growing within him.

Seren suppressed the elation that welled up within her. It was too soon, she reminded herself. There was still so much that could go awry.

She slowly closed the lid on the box. After a moment, Geraint stopped humming and simply stared first at the box and then at Seren.

"What does this mean?" he asked finally.

"Come and sit," Seren said, indicating the eating mat which was strewn with fresh cushions. A plate of dates was set invitingly in the center.

Geraint followed and sat opposite Seren. He waited for Seren to take a date, then chose one and nibbled at it.

"I believe you have the Talent to work with crystal," she said. "That means you hear the crystal. It also means you might be able to use it to magnify your thoughts or see the threads of life."

"But what does that mean?"

"The crystal is the tool of the Guardians."

His eyes grew large. "Does that mean I am to be a Guardian?"

"I do not know," she replied. "And even if you have the ability, there is a small problem."

"Because I am a dhavara," he said.

"No. Because you are male."

Seren bit into another date while the boy sat with that thought.

"No Guardian has ever been male." She wasn't about to tell him about the prophesy or that one version said that the Khevira could be male. The ancients had warned against revealing too much in case the knowledge altered the necessary path of the Protector of the Dhervina.

"It is also too soon to know how strong your Talent is," she said. "Did you just begin hearing the crystal?"

"Is that what I've been doing?"

She nodded. "Yes. You just came of age?"

He nodded. "This is my thirteenth summer."

"The ability is just now beginning to show itself. It will take many summers to grow into its final form."

"So what do I do?"

"I will have to speak with the other Guardians," Seren said. "If they agree, then you will begin training with me. You will learn how to master your ability and we will see what happens."

"What about my family?"

"Your sister is pledged to the Khutulun, so she is no longer your concern. As to your parents, you may see them on occasion. But the training will take a great deal of your energy and time."

"What is it you want me to do?" he asked.

"Go to your tent and bring back your things as quickly as you can. I will send word to the other Guardians and call for a consultation. They must approve your training. If they agree, you will join my tent and travel with me." What Seren did not say was that whether the others agreed or not, she was going to work with this boy. She had never encountered a Talent as strong as his seemed to be.

"When?"

"If they agree, you will join me immediately."

Once the boy had gone, Seren called to Pryderi.

When her handmaid stepped back inside, Seren recited the words calling for an urgent meeting. "You are to say this to each of the other Guardians. They need to hear this immediately. Tell them I will arrive as soon as I receive their confirmation. Quickly."

ANDRAS

"You will join my tent and travel with me."

Shocked, Andras hurried away from the Guardian's tent before she could feel his presence. He knew the Guardian could tell what he was thinking and would try to stop him. Not until he was far enough away did Andras feel it safe to think about what he had heard.

Having a dhavara within the Dhervina was bad enough. Training him to be a Guardian was unthinkable. It would make a mockery of the Guardians to allow that misshapen vessel of ayna'al to participate in the ceremonies or walk at the head of the Processions.

Not to mention being at audiences with the Great Khagan who always had a Guardian with him. The thought of that dhavara putting himself over the rest of the Dhervina was intolerable.

The dhavara had lost him the girl he wanted. To reward him was more than Andras could bear. Andras felt as if he was going to be violently ill.

He had to do something.

But what?

Andras had never had to single-handedly forestall a disaster. The Guardians and the Dheren were supposed to do that. But they were in league with the very ayna'al they were supposed to prevent.

He wandered back towards his family's tent.

He had to come up with something.

"Andras! Wait! Andras!"

The piping voice broke in on Andras' thoughts and he turned to see his betrothed's little brother, Deryn, waving as he ran towards him.

"Can you take me to see the races?" he asked. "Amma and Appa cannot and I am not allowed to go on my own."

Yorath and his wife arrived a moment later. She looked harassed and his future allianced father looked as if he would be anywhere but here.

"It would be my pleasure," Andras said, smiling at his betrothed's parents. "I will make sure he comes to no harm."

"Vinaka," Manari Celyn said, gratitude writ large on her worn face. "The Great Khagan is coming shortly and the servants are all needed to prepare. You have our true gratitude."

"I will enjoy becoming better acquainted with my new family," Andras said. Then he turned to his allianced father. "Manan Yorath," he said. "Perhaps I might speak with you upon my return. I have a matter upon which I would have your advice."

"Of course," Yorath said.

Andras put his hand out and took the boy's hand. "Come, Deryn. Lets go see the races."

BRYS

After the morning meal, Brys went in search of the slave who had befriended her brother.

She was glad of the errand as she wanted to see for herself what kind of person this woman was. Most importantly, she wanted to see if this woman spoke truly. If it was true that other dhavara lived among the Duta'ut, then she would not have to worry about him any longer. The thought of Geraint living among others like him was very pleasing to her.

She went by the pool first, but saw no one there who had hair of fire. She then made her way to the tent that had caused so much speculation and trouble. She had given the matter a great deal of thought since last evening. It was unlikely anyone of this tent would know she was the dhavara's sister, so she could approach the tent without causing trouble for the woman. But she also did not want to make anyone wonder why she was really there. If this woman could help Geraint, she did not want to cause her any difficulty.

The woman sweeping near the tent flap had dark hair. Brys watched for a little while, but no one else came or went. Finally Brys went up to the dark haired woman.

"I have heard that a woman with hair the color of fire rides with you," she said.

The woman stopped her sweeping and looked at Brys, her face changing from disgruntled to an expressionless mask.

"You cannot see her now. That one is being ridden by the manan."

Brys looked at the woman, curiosity getting the best of her. "You do not like her."

The woman gave her a look of disgust. "All the women share a tent, but she is allowed to sleep in her own tent. Only the manan is allowed to ride her while the rest of us must take whatever rider comes. She has many nights when she can sleep without being ridden. The others, we have no such untroubled nights."

"You cannot say that you will not lie with someone?" Brys was shocked. All Dhervina women had the right to refuse.

"We are not Dhervina," the woman reminded her. "Yorath is a great one for talking about Dhervina law and tradition, but it does not extend to his slaves." The woman spat. "It would not be so bad if he rode all of us, but to allow his men to use us as they want is another thing."

"Why have you told me this?" Brys asked. "I could inform Yorath of your words and then he would punish you."

"But you will not," the woman said, a knowing look on her face. "You are Khutulun. So you understand. And even if you did inform, it would not change anything. He would make me lie with all of them as punishment, but even that would be nothing new."

"Protection for all is the Dhervina code," Brys protested. "It should cover all who ride with us."

"But it does not." The woman spat again.

"Would you become Khutulun if you could?" Brys asked, not knowing if it was even permitted.

"Anything to get away from this tent," she said. "But I doubt it is allowed."

"I do not know," Brys admitted. "But you could always ask."

The woman stared off into the distance as if considering Brys' words. Then shrugged. "Vinaka for your words, Khutulun. Perhaps I shall."

A sharp cry cut through the noise of the Tanaiste from beyond Yorath's tent. Brys and the woman looked in that direction. Brys did not see anything, but the woman grimaced.

"It would seem the manan has finished his ride. The woman you seek will be going to draw water soon and then you can see her hair."

"Is it truly the color of fire?" Brys asked.

"It is."

"That will be something to see," Brys said. "Vinaka for your assistance. I pray the gods of your people will watch over you."

"Hah!" The woman spat again. "That would be the first time since I was captured, but from your lips to their ears." She then began sweeping again vigorously.

Assuming Yorath was about to come out of the tent, Brys turned away, not wanting him to see her face.

She strolled down the thoroughfare looking at the displays with feigned interest as she kept watch for Rhian.

When she finally caught sight of her, Brys was shocked. While her hair was indeed as red as fire, it was not the only colorful thing on her. Her face was badly bruised with colors of black, blue, red, and green. She was walking slowly as if it was an enormous effort to go even one step further, yet she continued to walk, the water skins at her sides looking as if they were anvils.

Brys moved forward without thinking and took the skins from the woman's hands.

"I will carry these for you, Rhian," she said. Then, before the woman could say anything, Brys leaned in and whispered, "My brother asked me to visit you."

Rhian looked at her with exhausted eyes. "Your brother?"

"Geraint of Halaka," Brys said quietly.

"Did Yorath visit him, as well?" Rhian asked.

Brys helped her sit on a boulder that formed part of the wall surrounding the pool.

"He did," Brys said. "But the Guardian was there, so Yorath had no opportunity to harm him."

"I am glad. I wanted to warn him, but was unable."

"Geraint also wanted to warn you," Brys said. "But it looks as if I am too late."

Rhian shrugged. "Yorath learned your brother visited his tent and beat me for allowing it before he went to visit your brother. So it was always too late. But if it had not been that, Yorath would have found some other excuse to beat me. It makes him feel more powerful."

"Yet you lie with him," Brys observed.

Brys let out a short sound too ugly to be a laugh.

"You think I have a choice?" She laughed again. "He is the manan and I do as he commands if I want to keep my skin."

So it was true.

Brys shook her head. "My heart hurts that this is so," she said quietly. "I did not know this about the Dhervina."

"You are yet young," Rhian said. "You will learn much as you add more summers to your life. Now I must finish getting the water and return or Yorath will wonder where I have gone and then will beat me again or ride me yet again and I am in much pain. He is a very suspicious man."

"I have a message for you from my brother," Brys said. "Then I will help you with the water."

"You are very kind," Rhian said, wincing as she shifted her seat on the rock.

Brys shook her head. "No. But you were kind to my brother and I owe you a deep debt of gratitude for that."

"He is an unusual boy," Rhian said. "He was the first to talk to me as if I was a manari and not some Duta'ut slave." She looked away and Brys wondered if she was about to weep. "What is the message?"

"He said to tell you that he would visit if he could, but he's been ordered to stay away from Yorath's tent. He also does not want to cause you more trouble and hopes he may be of assistance one day. He asks your forgiveness for causing you trouble and wishes you well."

"Will you tell him I enjoyed speaking with him? Now I really must return to Yorath's tent."

Brys filled the skins with water and carried them back to Yorath's tent. Fortunately he was not there when they returned, so Brys was able to carry the skins all the way to the water containers and fill them.

She bid Rhian farewell and then made her way to the Khutulun camp. She had delivered Geraint's message, but her heart was troubled by what she had learned. After what Rhian had told her, Brys was doubly determined to join the Khutulun. She had no desire to be ridden against her will.

SEREN

As the youngest of the Guardians, Seren was obliged to make the long journey up the valley to the tent of the senior Guardian whose tent was set in the northern most part of the valley. It took Seren much longer to make her way all that distance than she had expected.

She had forgotten that the dhavara was unable to walk as quickly as she. When she realized her error, she made a detour to where his horse was tethered so he could ride.

He showed her how to skirt the encampment to avoid the crush of the thoroughfare and curious eyes, but by the time Seren entered the tent of Guardian Myared, the other Guardians had already taken their places on the East and West stations on the circle surrounding the Place of Honor. Myared was seated on her cushion at the North end.

Myared, the Guardian for Kypchak Ulshyn, and the eldest, had been a Guardian long before Seren had shown signs of crystal Talent. She was surrounded by numerous cushions to help her sit. Seren had heard that she was now having difficulty moving at all.

The power of the crystal could only extend life for so long. Once it ceased being effective, the decline was cruel. The only boon was that death came quickly. Seren had seen her predecessor go from healthy and vital to a body twisted and bent within a few cycles of the moon before she died in terrible pain.

Watching her suffer had made Seren decide that she would have the Khutulun brew her a strong essence of nightshade when that time came.

Now Seren stepped forward and took her place at the south end of the circle in the center of the tent. She had left Geraint to wait outside the tent until the ritual had been conducted and the matter discussed.

Myared gestured to two handmaidens standing nearby. They came forward quickly and assisted the Guardian to her feet and helped her to the circle. Rather than withdrawing as was custom, they remained, their hands under Myared's arm to help her stand.

Seren was shocked at how far the other Guardian had deteriorated since she had last seen her. She wondered if Myared could even last the length of the Tanaiste. To die during the Tanaiste would be seen as an omen of coming ostuda. That would be most unfortunate at this particular Tanaiste given the presence of Geraint and the ill feelings already running like wild fire through the valley.

Once Myared was in place, a handmaiden for each Guardian stepped forward with the boxes containing the four large crystals belonging to the Dhervina. One for each Kypchak.

Each opened their box and withdrew the crystals with both hands. As they did, the crystals began to glow. The handmaidens stepped away with the now empty boxes.

The Guardians then stepped forward into the center of the carpet. Seren placed her crystal against that of the crystal from the the East, matching two sides. The western Guardian then added her crystal so that there was now a much larger crystal with a piece missing on the end.

The three turned, all having the same thought, but Myared gestured to them to stay where they were. She tottered forward and slid her crystal into place, completing the circle. The larger crystal now began to glow with greater intensity.

Myared stepped back slightly, unable to complete the next step.

The other three lowered the huge crystal of the Dhervina into place on the carpet at the center of the circle.

The carpet itself was ancient. While it did not go back to the time of the beginning, it had been woven over ten thousand summers before.

All four colors of the kypchaks were woven into it, but the once vibrant colors had dimmed and the thread of the warp now showed through in places. It was said that when the carpet could no longer serve, it was a sign that the Time of Destruction was at hand.

The women stepped back and sat on their cushions, now ready to discuss the matter that had brought them together. It took a few moments for Myared to get settled, but finally her handmaidens withdrew and they could speak freely.

All were dressed in ordinary clothes of black pants and tunics with white ribbons in their hair.

"So what has happened?" Myared asked, her voice rusty and cracked.

Seren was appalled that even Myared's beautiful voice had been taken. *How is she able to activate the crystal?* The Guardian's voice was second only to the power of her mind. More importantly, certain powers of the crystal could only be activated by using the voice.

"The prophecy says, "The Khevira will be unlike any other," Seren began. "I believe that the Khevira is Geraint of family Tumen, kereit Halaka, Kypchak Kishyn. A dhavara."

When no one said anything, she told them of her encounter with the dhavara and described what she had seen in the vision.

"You believe he has crystal Talent?" Myared asked. "But you have no proof of that as yet."

"No. But if he is the Khevira, it would be a mistake to leave him where he is and hope everything will turn out well. It is clear he is in serious danger from the other Dhervina."

"So what do you propose?" Urien asked. Urien was the Guardian of Kypchak Orshyn which rode to the east and protected the remains of their traditional homeland from the Sarkinen. The warriors of Kypchak Orshyn had become the fiercest warriors of all the Dhervina because of constant attacks by the Sarkinen who wanted nothing more than to destroy all Dhervina completely.

Urien had the sharp features and lean body of the Eastern Dhervina and she always seemed on edge, as if she was expecting an attack from behind at any moment.

"With the agreement of the Guardians, I will take him in and train him," Seren told them. "I will then be able to watch him closely. In another summer or two, we will have an answer." She looked at the others quizzically. "Do you see a better course of action?"

"And this vision of fire and ash? You believe this is what will happen if he stays where he is. What if it predicts what will happen if you take him in and train him?"

This question came from Wynne, the Guardian of the West. Where Urien was lean, Wynne was plump. She had round features and a face that never seemed to stop smiling. It sometimes made Seren wonder what the other woman was truly thinking.

"I did consider that," Seren said. "As I felt the same thing when I touched his sister, I believe the two are linked. I believe the fire is what will happen if he stays with his family. It could also be a forewarning of the Time of Destruction."

"What of the Dheren?" Urien wanted to know. "Will they make him a full member?"

"Yes," Seren said. "I have spoken to the Dheren and they see no reason he should not be confirmed as full Dhervina."

"If you leave him where he is," Wynne asked. "You believe he will be killed. If he is a dhavara, is that perhaps not a good thing?"

"Not if he is the Khevira of the prophecy," Seren said. "And we cannot know that for at least two summers."

"As I seem to recall," Myared said. "Dhavaras were not always considered ostuda. At one time, it was said that they *prevented* ostuda. And the prophesy tells us, 'They will be unlike the people. They will be set apart.'" She peered at them, her gaze sharp as it went from one to the next. "And does not the prophesy say that the Time of Destruction will begin after twelve thousand summers? It has been nearly that now."

Seren nodded along with the others.

"But the second moon has not yet made itself known," Wynne pointed out.

"It will take many summers for the Khevira to learn to harness the power of the crystal," Seren reminded them. "It would be disaster for the Dhervina should the second moon arrive before the Khevira is ready."

The others nodded.

"You believe this dhavara is the Khevira then," Myared said.

The others looked at her and then at Seren.

"I believe there is a good chance that this is so," Seren said cautiously. "There is always the chance that he is not. But if we refuse to train him because he is male, and the second moon arrives without another Talent of his potential, the Dhervina, and indeed all of our world, will be in peril."

"There is no doubt a male dhavara is unlike any other," Myared said. "But we should also continue to search for other Talent, as well."

She glanced at the other Guardians. "I believe I am not alone in my desire to meet this dhavara," she added.

The other Guardians nodded, their eyes revealing what their faces did not. This was a momentous occasion and all wished to lay their gaze upon someone who might well be the ancient prophecy fulfilled.

Seren opened the tent flap and beckoned Geraint in.

Geraint

Geraint worked hard to temper his excitement. Everything seemed to have changed in the swish of a horse's tail and it seemed to him he was in a dream that would vanish when he awoke. And this was one dream from which he did not want to awake.

Unable to sit patiently, he paced in a circle, trying to dissipate the nerves that threatened to overwhelm him. Every time he passed the tent flap, he looked for movement, but it remained closed with no hint of what was going on inside.

Finally, when he thought he might well perish from anticipation, the flap opened and Seren beckoned him inside.

He straightened his vest, brushed non-existent dust from his clothes and followed her inside.

When his eyes had adjusted to the dimly lit tent, he saw a very old woman surrounded by cushions. Seren walked Geraint right up to her.

"Guardian Myared, this is the boy I was telling you about," Seren said. Then she patted Geraint on the shoulder and stepped away.

Geraint saw the old woman peer at him with eyes that seemed to glitter.

The crystal is in her blood.

The thought came into his mind suddenly and he wondered how he knew that.

Then he felt her energy slip into his mind. It felt dry and ancient and thin and he knew she was dying. Yet underneath he could sense a deep well of knowledge and ancient wisdom and he felt himself drawn in to see more.

Then suddenly she was gone as if a tent flap had been quickly pulled closed. Geraint staggered slightly with shock.

"So you *do* have Talent," Guardian Myared said. "*Strong* Talent. Very interesting. You will go far, boy."

The old woman shifted her gaze to Seren who was standing behind him.

"You have seen well Guardian Seren," she said. "Ensure he receives proper training. Such a Talent should not be lost."

Then Seren was back at his side.

He looked at the old woman again, hoping to catch another glimpse of what he had felt, but his mind was met with a wall as cold and solid as the mountain. Yet her mouth twisted into what seemed to be a small smile and Geraint had the feeling she was pleased.

Then Seren put her hand on his shoulder.

As he turned, he saw a huge crystal in the middle of the tent. It looked as if it was on fire.

He didn't have a chance to stare before he was back outside the tent.

"Why did the crystal look like it was on fire?" Geraint asked. He had never seen it do that before.

"The crystal glows in the presence of Talent. The more Talent there is, the more it glows," she said. "The Guardians have strong Talent."

Geraint wondered if he would one day be able to set the Crystal on fire in that manner. That would be a wondrous thing indeed, he thought as he climbed the ladder up to his saddle.

If he had that kind of power, he would never need fear anyone again.

SEREN

Seren tried to hold her elation in check as she retraced her steps to her tent. But despite countless summers of training, she found it difficult to remain calm.

First there had been the reaction of the Great Crystal to Geraint's presence. She had not told Geraint the entire truth. It did glow in the presence of Talent, but never anything like *that*.

And his full talent hasn't even manifested yet.

She thought of the way she would be received by the Great Khagan when it become known she had found and trained the Khevira. And how the Dhervina from all the kereits would honor her when the Gate had once again been sealed.

It would make up for the summers of grueling training and going without sleep. It would even make up for being scorned for having the smallest, most vulnerable kypchak.

With the Khevira at her side, she would command the highest respect.

And to be the one who found the Gate once again! The thought made her head reel as if she was on an untamed horse.

By the time she arrived at her tent, Seren was in an excellent mood.

"Once you have set up the boy's sleeping mat and the other things he will need, you may both enjoy the Tanaiste until the sun's light fades from the valley," she told her handmaidens expansively. "We will have much work to do once Geraint begins his training."

She took on the task of showing Geraint where he would sleep and began preparing him for the training that would begin before the sun's light rode into the valley.

"This path is not for the faint hearted," she told him. "But if you work hard, you have the potential to become one of the greatest Guardians the Dhervina have ever seen."

YORATH

Yorath kept his face a mask of stone as he listened to Andras tell him what he had overheard from the Guardian's tent.

"At the end, she said, 'You will join my tent and travel with me,'" Andras said at the end of his recital. "So you can see why I had to speak to you."

Yorath wanted to rage or run a sword through something, but pulled the bridle on his emotions. It would not do to show weakness to anyone, especially his son-to-be.

"You did well to come to me," Yorath said instead. "The thought of that dhavara putting himself over the rest of the Dhervina is intolerable." The words flew out like thrusting spears in battle.

"Is there anything we can do?"

"There is always something that can be done," Yorath said. "But what that is to be, requires a great deal of thought. This is the Tanaiste and we have our position and reputation to consider."

Yorath was feeling better about the boy who was to join his family. When his daughter had insisted that she would only consider Andras for an alliance, Yorath had been opposed. The wealth of the family was in the boy's favor, but he had seen little else that might bring his family an increase in wealth or power.

When Andras had approached him, he had thought it was to be on some trivial thing. The seriousness of the matter had caused him to rethink his judgment. The boy might be a useful addition to the family, after all, especially since he shared Yorath's beliefs on the dhavara.

Additionally, if Yorath took action against the dhavara, then his own reputation could only increase.

RHIAN

Ever since the beating, Rhian had done her utmost to stay out of Manan Yorath's vision. She knew his temper would re-ignite if she made even a small misstep. She had additionally been blessed that he had not sought her out in her tent for yet another punishing ride. The flesh in her womanly area was still tender and she prayed he would remain away or use one of the other woman until his rage subsided.

As soon as she finished serving the evening meal, she slipped into the tent of supplies. It was one of the few times she could count on having no one watching her.

Since arriving in the valley, Rhian had gradually hidden small packets of dried food in an unused basket. Now she added one last bag of dried meat and dragged the basket out of the back of the tent and into a hidden corner.

Later, once the family was settled for the night, she went out as if to go to the tent of necessity. Moving quickly, she retrieved the basket and hoisted it onto her back. It was heavier than she had anticipated and Rhian staggered slightly, but then found her balance. She winced as the basket pressed upon a bruise and she had to take a few precious moments to ease it to a less sensitive place. Then she headed to the south end of the valley.

The moon was barely peering over Khurilar, the eastern peak, when she began, but blessedly it was high by the time she finally cleared the last of the tents.

The pass was more barren than she expected and it took some time before she encountered a jumble of huge rocks. She squeezed behind a particularly large one and found a place for the basket where it would not be visible from the pass even on horseback.

On the last night of the Tanaiste, she would take a horse and tether it there, as well. Manan Yorath would not miss one or two horses for some time. The difficulty would be finding the time to slip away without being seen.

When she started back, Rhian saw with dismay that the moon had traveled nearly across the sky. If anyone woke and noticed her missing, there would be trouble. To ensure her safety, Rhian scratched her leg and arms with a sharp stone and slipped a small stone into her right sandal to increase her limp.

When she arrived at the tent, Rhian was brought up sharply by the sight of Yorath waiting outside her tent.

Her heart began pounding like a war drum.

How long had he been there? Had he seen her take the basket? She silently thanked the gods of her people for giving her the wisdom to prepare an excuse.

"Manan," she said. She was unable to read his face even with the moon's light still bathing the valley.

Of all nights for him to come to her tent.

"You have been gone for some time," Yorath said, his voice ominously quiet.

"I went to the tent of necessity further up the valley," she said.

"Why to that one?"

"It is cleaner and there are fewer young warriors to trouble me." All of which was true. The tent of necessity nearer this tent was much used by the warriors of the Khirgis. She had never returned there after seeing and smelling the condition.

"Yet you should have returned much sooner."

"Someone ran into me, knocking me down." She showed him the scratches on her arm. "It took a long time to walk back as the fall injured my foot."

"I see."

"Manan..."

"You know I do not permit my servants to have relations with others," he said.

She gaped at him in shock. *Is that what he though she was doing?* A sound that was half laugh, half gasp escaped her.

"I beg your pardon, Manan, but that is the last thing I would do. I have no interest in the other men of the Dhervina."

"I would see for myself," he said roughly.

He spun her around and lifted her skirt, pushing her forward until she was facing the ground. A moment later his member was pushing into her.

Rhian put a knuckle in her mouth and bit hard to keep from crying out. It would only inflame him and make it worse. He would be done soon enough. And the pain would eventually subside. She only hoped this would be the last time he would be able to use her. If only she could take a knife to his throat before she left.

But she had seen what the Dhervina did to murderers who were Dhervina. It would likely be worse for her as she was no Dhervina. She was Duta'ut, the Other. More, she was a slave. Punishment would be far harsher. Especially as Yorath was her owner. She had heard and seen too much since being captured to chance it.

Finally he was finished and allowed her to cover herself.

"I see you spoke truly," he said. "See that you are in your tent when I come for you again."

"Manan," Rhian said meekly, her gaze firmly on the ground. It had blessedly grown darker and her face was in shadow, masking her rage and resentment.

She could feel him scrutinizing her and she prayed he had seen nothing that would give away her plan. But finally he left and she was able to return to her sleeping mat.

She washed herself and made sure to use the herbs to prevent pregnancy that she had gotten from the healer. Especially now when she was so close to making her escape. The thought of his child in her belly made her nauseous.

Neiren

When Neiren entered the Guardian's tent, his gaze was drawn to the dhavara standing at the Guardian's side. He had not expected to see the boy here. Let alone standing next to the Guardian as if he belonged there.

"Neiren of Family Darligyn, kereit Malika, Kypchak Kishyn," he said automatically, his mind on how to ask the dhavara to leave in a way that would not insult the Guardian.

"Welcome Dheren Neiren of Malika," the Guardian replied. "Will you partake of tea?"

"My apologies to your guest," Neiren said with a nod to the boy. "But I must speak with you on a matter of great delicacy."

The Guardian did not answer immediately, but scrutinized Neiren through narrowed eyes. Then, as if receiving an answer, she bent down and whispered something to the boy.

The dhavara looked at Neiren, then back at Seren. He bowed slightly and left the tent.

"Would you care to sit and take some tea now?" Seren asked.

"I will," Neiren said. He waited for the Guardian to sit and then did the same.

Neiren waited patiently while the tea was poured and the handmaidens dismissed.

"I was surprised to see the dhavara at your side this day, Guardian," he began cautiously.

"Geraint is in training with me," she told him, her face and voice calm.

As if it was a matter of no importance.

"My heart grows heavy with that knowledge," Neiren said. "I wish to speak with you about his presence among the Dhervina." Neiren wondered how much she was able to sense as he tried to find the right words.

"I understood that the Dheren had no objection to confirming the boy as Dhervina," the Guardian said.

"That seems to be the case," Neiren confirmed. "But that has not yet occurred."

He leaned forward to communicate his concern. "I am not convinced that the Dhervina will be well served by his continued presence."

"And why is that, Dheren Neiren?"

Her manner was much too calm and it made Neiren's palms grow moist.

"It has become increasingly clear that the Dhervina are unlikely to accept him even if the Council of Dheren confirm the boy. My concern is that if we allow him to become full Dhervina, the people will lose all respect for the law."

"The law or the Dheren?" Seren asked, her tone sharp.

"Both. It is unfortunate and unfair, but I have become convinced that the boy should leave. Both for his safety and to protect the Dhervina. If he does not leave, I believe the people will act on their own to make him leave. I have also come to believe that he will not leave the valley alive unless he does so on his own. And soon."

The Guardian's face gave nothing away and Neiren wondered if she understood the import of what he was saying.

"Why do you come to me?" she asked finally after the silence had grown almost too heavy for Neiren to bear.

"Two reasons," he said. "The first is in the hope that perhaps you have seen something that will indicate what might happen."

"And the second?"

"To use your influence to persuade the Council to reject the dhavara and ask him to leave the valley immediately."

Her face seemed made of stone.

Neiren leaned forward again.

"I have no personal aversion to the boy," he said as urgently as possible. "But I believe this to be necessary to save both the boy and the Dhervina."

"And if I were to tell you that he is likely the Khevira of the prophesy? What would you say then?"

He leaned back in surprise. Of all the things he thought she would say, bringing up the prophesy was not one of them.

"Truth be told, I do not believe in the prophesy," he said after considering the matter. "It is a legend from the homeland we lost to the Sarkinen many thousands of summers past. And even if it is true, I do not believe it will change what is going to happen if the dhavara stays."

The Guardian gazed at him for a long time. Then she inclined her head slightly.

"I will think on your words very carefully," she told him.

"May I inquire as to whether you have seen what is to be?" he asked.

"What I have seen is not yet clear to me," she admitted. "But what I do know is that the boy has a rare talent that should not be wasted or lost to the Dhervina. The chance that he is the Khevira is very strong."

"Can you offer me anything?" Neiren asked.

"All I can do for now is think upon your words." The Guardian put up her hand to indicate he should not yet arise. "I rely on your discretion not to mention the possibility of the boy being the Khevira. I only mentioned it to you so you would understand the difficulty of what you are asking. It is not something that should become known among the Dhervina."

"You can rely on my discretion, as always, Guardian Seren," he replied.

As he returned to his tent, Neiren considered what the Guardian had said. Would it make a difference if the boy was the promised Khevira?

He was enough of a traditional Dhervina for the words of the Prophesy and the idea of the Khevira to affect him deeply. Then he shook his head and dismissed the idea. It would not change what he knew to be in the hearts of the Dhervina. Khevira or not, the boy should go.

BRYS

Idris was waiting when Brys arrived at the Khutulun encampment. When Brys would have greeted her, she put her hand to her lips to indicate silence and then led Brys through the Khutulun camp.

Brys followed as they wound their way through the camp. Brys had thought the tents were set in a great circle, but now saw they were not. They were walking in a circle, but one that grew smaller and smaller. Instead of ending at the beginning, it simply went deeper into the encampment.

As Brys walked, it seemed to her as if she was traveling a great distance beyond the valley of the Tanaiste. The further she went into the encampment, the quieter it seemed to get.

All the tent flaps were closed and the camp felt as if it had been deserted. Voices from outside became muffled the further she went. Even the air itself seemed denser and hushed, as if it was early dawn instead of full day.

Brys felt as if she had been carried to another place by the time she reached the large tent that felt as if it was in the center of the Khutulun encampment.

When they reached the tent, Idris smiled and squeezed Brys' hand and then was gone, leaving Brys to enter alone. She looked around one last time at the blazing sky and the colors of the tents around her. She thought of Geraint and her parents and wished them well. She knew that when she came out of the tent, she would be changed.

She faced forward, took a deep breath, and entered the tent.

The inside of the tent was dark and warm. She had thought it would be cool, but a brazier had been lit and the air was hazy with smoke. Brys looked up and saw that the hole at the top was very small, trapping much of the smoke inside. Hangings had been used to create a private area of the back of the tent so the central area was much smaller than it might have been.

Six other girls stood inside the tent. All were looking around, confusion vying with curiosity on their faces.

A moment later, the tent flap opened and then closed. Kheran Esyllt strode to the center of the tent and stood near the brazier. This time she was dressed in the clothes of a warrior – a plain red vest, riding pants and sandals. Her arms were bare and well muscled as if she had worked a thousand horses. But it was difficult to see her face as the only light came from the burning brazier.

She clapped her hands three times and then pointed to a half circle set out in red on the carpet that surrounded the brazier. Brys moved closer and stood on the line with the others.

"I am Kheran Esyllt," she said. "I am the Kheran responsible for all of you until you have completed your training. You will keep silence during this ceremony unless I ask you a question. You must use the silence to hear your true heart and consider what it is you are undertaking.

"Do not be wondering about the other girls who are here, or thinking about what you look like or any other trivial matter. This is the time when you must concern yourself only with your change from girl to Khutulun."

She paused and looked at each girl in turn, her gaze searching. "Khutulun is a sacred calling. It is not a riding vest to be taken off if it does not fit. It is your life and you will spend the rest of it with us. You will obey all things Khutulun. You must never, upon pain of death, divulge anything you see or experience over the next three days. You must never divulge anything about the Khutulun to anyone who is not Khutulun.

"If you disagree with something or see something about which you have a question, you will come to me directly. I am the Kheran of the new Khutulun. If you are still unsatisfied, you may speak with the Kheran of all the Khutulun.

"But obedience to the Khutulun and the High Kheran is paramount."

She looked at each of them again. "Are you willing to abide by the laws of the Khutulun?"

"I am," Brys answered along with the others.

"The laws of the Khutulun come before all others. Do you agree to abide by this?"

"I do," they all said.

"Are you willing to leave your old life behind and take on the new life of the Khutulun?"

"I am," Brys answered evenly. The question was asked of the others and each girl answered the same in turn.

"Remove your clothing and place it in the basket behind you. As you shed your clothing, so you shed the life you once knew. It is like the snake that sheds its skin so it can grow. You will see a red shift on the basket. Put it on. It will keep you warm during this time."

Along with the other girls, Brys removed all of her clothing and placed it in the basket and slipped the shift over her head before returning to her place on the circle. The shift was thin and she was glad of the heat in the tent.

Now seven women entered from the back area of the tent. They were also dressed as for battle and were carrying shears. Each stood behind one of the girls.

"Are you willing to cut away that which you were in order to become Khutulun?" the Kheran asked.

"I am."

"We cut your hair to symbolize your willingness to do so."

The Kheran nodded at the other women.

Brys felt the woman behind her draw close and then felt the tug on her hair as it was cut. Soon the weight of her hair was gone. The red ribbons tickled her shoulders. She wanted to put her hand up to see how much was left, but refrained in case it was forbidden.

The women returned to the back of the tent with the hair, but returned almost immediately. They were each carrying a tray with a cup and a small morsel of food. Each woman stood in front of a girl.

"To indicate your willingness to live with us and be one with us, I invite you to partake of the sacred tea and food."

Brys bit into the small package on her tray. It was meat cooked and wrapped in grape leaves. She then drank the tea in one gulp. Even so, it was bitter and she fought to keep it in her stomach.

"Here you will remain until tomorrow. When the light from the sun reaches Khurtagin we will come for you.

"You will use this time to keep watch. To think upon your true heart and consider it as you become Khutulun.

"You will have visions as you keep watch. You must embrace these visions. They will show you something that will become a part of you and guide you upon your path. This guide may be in the form of an animal or something else. It may be a weapon. It may only be a horse or a blade of grass. Whatever it is, you will know it.

"Then you must remember your guide. It will be easy to get distracted and lose your grasp upon it as you journey through the lands of the shadow.

"If you lose it, you could lose your way and never reach the final tent of the Khutulun on the far side."

Brys was finding it difficult to keep her eyes open. The heat from the brazier enveloped her and the light from the candles seemed to double. The Kheran's voice seemed to come and go in waves and the sense of her words began to get lost. She tried to concentrate, but finally all she felt were warm hands holding her arms and laying her down on the thick carpets.

GERAINT

The next three days were the happiest of Geraint's life.

Seren woke him even before the sun's light reached the valley. She had him dress warmly and brought him into the main tent.

An ornately carved box sat on a low pedestal in the center of the tent, illuminated by a myriad of flickering candles. The rest of the tent lay in darkness and Geraint felt himself drawn closer. The air in the tent seemed hushed and Geraint felt as if he were in the heart of the valley, as well as far away at the same time. He thought he smelled oranges, but then the scent was gone.

"The Great Crystal of Kypchak Kishyn rests in that box." Seren's voice was low as if to avoid waking it. "There are three other such crystals," she added. "Each Kypchak has one. When we are all together, our crystals fit together and become one enormous crystal. You saw it when you were examined yesterday. The Great Crystal must always rest in the exact center of the tent. It is the Place of Honor and reminds us that the Crystal is the center, the heart of the Dhervina. It is our power."

She led Geraint up to the Place of Honor. He was pleased to see the pedestal was low enough for him to be able to reach into the box. He had been concerned that everything would be too high and he would look foolish.

Seren stood squarely in front of the box.

"You must always open the box and carry the Crystal with both hands," she told him as she opened the box. "This creates a circle and the energy of the crystal will begin to flow. If you only use one hand, the energy cannot flow. It will build up within you and will kill you. The stronger your Talent, the stronger the energy."

Geraint nodded, awed that he was even allowed to touch the crystal.

Seren carried the crystal to one of the cushions nearby and seated herself on the larger one. Geraint sat on the other, unable to take his eyes off the Crystal.

Then he realized he could not hear the hum. He stared at the Crystal and then at Seren.

"I cannot hear it," he told her.

"That is of no matter," she said with a flap of her hand. "You are just now coming into your Talent," she said. "The ability will come and go for some time. Once you are older, the ability will always remain if you keep training."

Geraint took a deep breath of relief. He had been afraid that he had already lost the ability and she would make him leave.

"Before the sun rises, I activate the crystal and make certain that I am in tune with it. Then I see what energies flow throughout the camp. During the Tanaiste, I search the entire valley."

"What about the other Guardians?" Geraint asked. "Do they not do the same?"

"They do," she said. "But we all have different strengths. I see things that they do not, and they see others that I do not. During the Tanaiste, there are so many Dhervina that all of us are needed to keep difficulties at bay."

"What do you see when you use the Crystal?" Geraint asked now.

"I see the threads of life," she said. "I see where the energy is dark. Then I know who needs my assistance to get things flowing once again. Sometimes I see images that tell what will happen and what has happened. My best gift is reading energy. I can tell what has happened when I enter someone's tent," she explained. "Then I remove the bad energy and replace it with good before it does more harm."

"How do you do that?"

"I remove bad energy with the crystal and often use bells, clapping and salt," she said. "But I will tell you more of this later. What you need to know now is that you will see many things. And sometimes you will dream of what is to come."

"How do you know what is now and what is to be?" Geraint asked.

"It is not always clear," Seren admitted. "Usually there is a feel of sharpness if it is now. The further away it is in time, the less clear it will seem."

"Are you able to predict the future, then?" That would be a wonderful thing, Geraint thought.

"A little," Seren said slowly. "But not always. So much can change. You can see where the energies are and what they might lead to. Even then things can change and the matters you thought would resolve a certain way end differently. So all we do is read the energies and see where they *might* lead."

"Oh." Geraint was disappointed. "I had hoped to know when Tegan and his friends are planning to waylay me so I could avoid them."

"Unfortunately it is not so easy or clear. Although in time you may get a feeling that warns you when something is to happen in the near future, but it can be difficult to know what or where or how."

She returned the large crystal to the box and closed it. Then she reached behind her neck and removed the crystal hanging there. She knelt next to him and held the cooper wire in both hands, the crystal dangling in the center. It was the size of a hen's egg and was clear.

"You will use this crystal to practice. It is small so it does not have the power of the large crystal. But it will help you hone your Talent and abilities. Later, when you work with the large crystal, you will be able to do more. You will wear this crystal at all times. Having it always with you will help you hear its energy. So you will be able to work with it."

She fastened the crystal around his neck.

Geraint winced in sudden pain as a thin shriek pierced his skull. He hummed a matching tone and the shriek dissolved.

"Very good," Seren said.

"Will that happen all the time?" Geraint hoped it would not. It was very uncomfortable.

"Only until you and the crystal are tuned into each other. When you hum, you align yourself to the crystal. Once you are in tune with the crystal, you will be able to direct the power of the crystal. And the more you work with the crystal, the more you will merge with it. You will become as the crystal and then the sound will lessen and, over time, will disappear.

"When you voice a command without the crystal, your words are heard and others may or may not obey them," she continued. "If you have power, then they obey. If you do not, they do not."

"Like the Great Khagan. He has the power of the Dhervina and all obey him," Geraint said.

Seren smiled. "Exactly. But with the crystal, all that is changed."

"Do all the crystals have the same sound?"

"No. Most are different." Seren pointed to the katra manara that hung from the peg.

Geraint had been too overcome during her visit to his tent to pay much attention to the vest. But now he saw that the bottom of the vest nearly touched the ground and was covered with crystals of different sizes and colors.

"Each of the crystals on the katra manara now sing in harmony with each other and with me," she said. "But when they were found, they were not in harmony."

She led him over to the vest and picked up the hem, then pointed to a crystal that looked as if it was made with gold.

"Many crystals have colors in them and sometimes it can be difficult to find their energy sound. A large part of your Talent has to do with the ability to hear the crystal. Your task as a Guardian is to find the sound of its energy."

"But do you not need this crystal?" Geraint asked. He felt strongly drawn to the crystal and hungered after it more than anything he had ever encountered. But he did not want to overstep this soon.

"I have many crystals that the Guardians of our kypchak have found over countless summers. Many are on my katra manara and I have several others that will serve, as well as the large crystal of the kypchak."

She returned to the center of the tent and sat on the cushions. Geraint followed suit, wondering how he would be able to remember everything she was telling him.

"You must practice every day. It is the only way to strengthen your Talent," she told him. "It is much like riding a horse. You cannot become a great rider if you only ride once. You must ride every day. So it is with the Crystal."

"There is one other thing you need to know about the Crystal," Seren added. "While you can use it to see the threads of life, you can also use it to lend power to your voice. When you are older and have learned to control the small crystal, I will teach you how to harness the power of the crystal with your voice. That requires great skill and absolute control. It can be extremely dangerous both to you and those around you."

"What about the large crystal?" he asked.

"You will not work with that crystal until you are older and have much more control," she told him. "It is very powerful and you could do a great deal of harm."

"How will I know if I am doing it right?"

"You will know."

"What do I do after I open my mind to the crystal?"

"At first, just see what happens and where it takes you. Later we will refine your skill. When you are older, you will be able to send your mind anywhere and feel the energies of the people in each place."

"Even in the tent of the Great Khagan?" Geraint's eyes widened at the thought.

"Even there," Seren said. "But that would not be good. The Guardian of Kypchak Ulshyn would be most displeased."

"She could tell I was there?"

"She is the most powerful Guardian we have," Seren said.

Tegan

Tegan stumbled as he climbed up the side of the mountain nearest the dhavara's tent. The slope was littered with rocks of every size and, at first, when he began to slide backwards, his hands found nothing to grab onto. But then he slid into a small tree and he latched on, regaining his balance just before he tumbled all the way down to the bottom.

He and the others had waited until nearly dark to make the ascent, but the going was trickier than expected.

Someone else slipped a few moments later and let out a yelp.

"Sssss." Tegan tried to see who had nearly given them away. "He'll hear you."

"There's too much noise down there for him to hear anything," Kelmon whispered back.

It was true. People were still celebrating, but Tegan didn't want to take any chances.

"If he comes outside, he'll wonder what's making the noise or why the rocks are sliding onto his feet."

"How far up do we have to go?" Jolan grumbled.

"We're nearly there," Tegan said, pointing to several large rocks that reared up in the dim light like a herd of fighting stallions.

"We'll be able to see everything from there," he said.

"And then what?" Kelmon and two others hadn't been there when they had come up with their plan earlier.

"Tonight we see when he returns to his tent and we find a place to take the tent. Then tomorrow night we drag the tent out of the valley. Whatever we do to the dhavara is then no longer in the sacred valley and we cannot be censured."

"What about the others?" Jolan asked.

"What others?"

"The girl and the parents."

Tegan flapped his hand as if swatting at the flies on his horse.

"The girl has gone Khutulun so she won't be there and I am told the parents are always visiting elsewhere. Only the dhavara will be in the tent."

As one they all turned to look down at the tents below. The dhavara's was easily seen from this vantage point.

"Why don't we simply grab him the next time he comes out and carry him out of the valley?"

"The tent is the home of the kha," Jolan said. "It must be outside the valley or we will be banned for violating the Tanaiste."

That said, they finished the climb and got into place. Tegan settled in. The rock, still warm from the heat of the day, warmed him as the last of the light fled from the valley.

GERAINT

On the second day, Seren told Geraint about the scattered crystals.

"Yesterday I told you of the four large crystals of the Kypchaks. Today you will learn of the crystals that were scattered."

"Is this one of those?" Geraint asked, his hand going to the crystal around his neck.

"Indeed," Seren said. "I discovered that crystal near Bredon, the town of thieves. It had found its way into a riverbed and called to me as I rode past. I was most fortunate to have discovered it. There was a storm two sun cycles later and it could have been washed away and might never have been found."

"Why were they scattered?"

"Ahhh." Seren looked past him as she considered the question. "Unfortunately, only fragments of the story remain. You know how the Sarkinen pushed us out of our ancestral lands to the east, yes?"

Geraint nodded.

"Many things were lost then. Not only part of our home. But also the Story Keepers." Again Seren looked away as if lost in thought.

"I have heard it said that once there was another Great Crystal that was broken up and scattered to keep it from the Sarkinen." She waved at her katra manara. "But, as you see, there are a great many crystals and we know there are many more. Too many to have been only one crystal."

"Were there many Great Crystals then?" Geraint asked.

Seren shrugged. "Possibly. Or perhaps there were many small crystals that were scattered to keep them out of the hands of our enemies. Small crystals are easier to hide. At the same time, a great many remain in the lands to the East. And because so many of the Story Keepers were lost, over the thousands of summers, their location has been forgotten. We know that many have been discovered by others and have been used for other things."

"What other things?"

"Jewelry. Decoration. Some are in public and others are hidden away. Finding them is not a simple task."

"So how can we find them?"

"You will hear them," Seren said. "They call to those with crystal Talent. When you hear them, then you can track them down."

"Why haven't you tracked them down yet?" Geraint asked.

"I have found many." Seren showed him the katra manara. "As did the Guardians before me. But these I found only because they made themselves known to me during our ride on the Great Circle."

She returned the vest to its peg. "As for the others, it is not yet time. Many are in our ancestral lands stolen by the Sarkinen a thousand summers ago. It is still not safe for us to travel there."

"So how do we find them?" Geraint was fascinated by the thought of thousands of crystals secreted away in so many places.

"We have been promised that at the right time, someone will come along who can make the journey through our ancient homeland to the East and gather the crystals together."

"But if we have not had these small crystals for so many summers, why do we need to find them now?" Geraint asked.

"Once, back in the time of the ancients, we faced annihilation by an enemy from without. There was terrible fighting. Many died."

"When the Sarkinen came?"

Seren shook her head. "No. This happened many thousands of summers before that."

Geraint couldn't begin to imagine how long ago that must have been.

"We discovered the power of the crystals then and used them to drive the enemy away. They came through a Gate and the ancients used the power of the crystals to seal the Gate so they could no longer break through. But the ancients left word that after twelve thousand summers, the seal on the Gate would crack and we would need to seal it again to keep the enemy out. The only way to seal the Gate is with the crystals."

She knelt and looked at him in the face. "*All of them.* The only way we will have enough power is if we have all the crystals. Not even the four Great Crystals are strong enough on their own. We must have them all."

"We have also been told that when the time is right, someone with great power, a Khevira, will come and be a Guardian. She will have the power to use all the crystals as if they are one. She will bring all the Guardians together and the combined power will seal the Gate."

"But how will she find the other crystals if she cannot go to the lands of the Sarkinen?" Geraint asked.

"I do not know," Seren confessed. "And I have not been able to see. I only know that when a second moon arrives in the sky, we must find the Gate and seal it."

"Where is the Gate?" Geraint asked. Surely it couldn't be that difficult to find.

"That is but one of the stories we have lost," Seren said. "We know it is in the mountains of the East at the edge of a great plain. At one time we had a fifth Guardian who was the Oracle of the Dhervina. When she become Oracle, she no longer rode with the Dhervina. She lives near a sacred cave in the East and is said to know the secret of the Gate. It is also said she is a Story Keeper and she may still know how to find the Gate."

Seren shrugged. "But I do not know if that is true any longer. It has been over a thousand summers since we have been to our home in the East. It may be that the Oracle still continues. Or it could be she and the sacred cave were destroyed by the Sarkinen. No one knows."

"If she is no longer there, then what will this Khevira do?" Geraint asked.

"Whoever this Khevira is will know what to do when the time is right," Seren said. "That is what has come down to us over thousands of summers. What is important for you, is that you become the strongest Guardian you can in order to be ready for the Time of Destruction. For it is foretold that there will be terrible troubles and destruction when the second moon arrives and you must be ready for it."

"When is this to be?"

"No one knows for certain," Seren said. "But the first Guardians let it be known that it would come after twelve thousand summers and it has been nearly that now. So it may well come in your lifetime. You must be ready."

NEIREN

All his fathers before him had been dheren and Neiren had grown up on the stories of decisions and law breakers and the changes in both over thousands of summers. It was an honorable kereit and he had always taken great pride in his duties.

On most occasions, Neiren enjoyed the give and take of the Council of Dheren. To match wits with the best minds of the Dhervina was like the potion of youth to him. But this summer was not like any other. Had the dhavara come of age on another summer, it would have been an easy matter. But to do so in the summer of the Tanaiste had created terrible complications and made his stomach burn.

As he entered the tent of the Council of Dheren, Neiren saw that many dheren had already arrived. Neiren greeted each of them, making his rounds so as to reach Ofyed last. The two had been friends since their first summer as dheren and Neiren valued his friend's wisdom and advice. Even better, Ofyed was the dheren for kereit Halaka, the one containing the dhavara.

"It is so good to see you again, Ofyed," Neiren greeted as he at last reached his old friend.

"And you," the other man replied. "Yet another Tanaiste and we are still here."

"I could almost wish it otherwise," Neiren said.

"The dhavara?"

Neiren nodded. "It is going to be difficult."

"Has he suddenly sprouted horns and sucked the blood from all the horses?"

"You would know better than I," Neiren grinned. "But it makes no difference. There have been complaints this summer. The boy visited kereit Jirgin and the tent belonging to Manan Yorath of Kypchak Ulyshyn. Normal things for a boy his age, but he is a dhavara and that makes it a serious matter."

"I very much doubt the Council will banish him," Ofyed said. "I have known the dhavara his entire life, and the boy has shown no sign of intending any ayna'al."

"And what of all those who complain?" Neiren asked.

"They are superstitious and their complaints have no merit."

"You dismiss them too easily," Neiren said, raising his voice slightly as he saw several of the other dheren draw closer.

"Visiting kereit Jirgin is hardly serious," Ofyed retorted.

"Agreed. But their fear and anger are hardly trivial. I suspect there will be bloodshed over the dhavara if he is confirmed."

"Bloodshed?" Dheren Aeron of kereit Alukhai was a small man whose hair had gone the color of snow. "At the Tanaiste?"

"Perhaps not during the Tanaiste," Neiren said. "But soon after at the latest. The majority of Dhervina are not likely to accept the dhavara no matter what we decide."

"They may not like it," Aeron said. "But they will accept our decision."

"I don't believe they will," Neiren countered. "And if they don't, that will undermine our authority. I believe it will eventually cause our destruction."

The moment the words were out of his mouth, Neiren wished to call them back. They made him sound like one of the madmen they occasionally saw raving on the streets in the towns of the Duta'ut.

"Destruction?" Aeron scoffed. "You see phantoms riding, Neiren. Affirming the boy as full Dhervina is hardly going to lead to destruction. Phaw." He flapped his hand and walked away.

Neiren's heart sank as he saw the others move away quickly, as well.

"You went too far," Ofyed said. "There may, indeed, be trouble, but destruction? Over something this small? We have survived war and attempted eradication by the Sarkinen. We have even been pushed out of our ancestral lands. But we are still Dhervina, the people of the Great Horse. Allowing a dhavara born of Dhervina parents cannot harm us."

Neiren gripped his friend's upper arm in the friendship gesture. "I truly hope your words become truth," he said. "But I fear that this time they will not. I am not a Guardian, but this summer I see more clearly. Tempers run hot even though the boy has done nothing. If he is confirmed as Dhervina...."

Neiren ran out of words and he released Ofyed's arm. He opened his hands in a gesture of resignation.

"We must share a cup of fermented mare's milk at the end of the Tanaiste," Ofyed said. "We can celebrate the continuation of the Dhervina."

"I will be most pleased to join you should that be the case," Neiren said.

Then the bronze bell called them to begin the Council and Neiren took his place on the circle.

They began with decisions made since the last Tanaiste where one person had objected to the decision and appealed to the Council. There were only a few and that went quickly.

Next, the important decisions of the past seven summers were reviewed and most were affirmed. Instances where the dheren had gone too far were modified and runners sent to notify the Dhervina involved. The dheren would be required to return their fee to ensure the dheren would not repeat his error.

As there had been many such decisions, the Council went late into the night, concluding only when it became clear fatigue was setting in and some were falling asleep.

In the morning they would finish that part of their business and then move on to those who had come of age since the last Tanaiste.

Those who had reached that age in the last seven summers had already been granted approval by the local dheren and it was mere formality to give final approval to those individuals.

Those who had come of age this summer were taken last. As Neiren returned to his tent, he realized that the matter of the dhavara would likely be held until the very last. That would give him time to persuade others to his side. With enough time, he might be able to avoid the trouble looming ahead.

Brys

Brys found herself standing on a vast plain. She was dressed in the riding clothes of a Khutulun and the ribbons in her hair tickled her shoulders.

In the distance, snow-capped mountains beckoned and she instinctively moved in that direction. They looked to be a great distance and she wondered if she would be able to reach them in time.

Yet even as she walked, the distance closed and she was soon in the foothills. A stream pelted down nearby.

Brys knelt, filled her hands with water and drank. The water was clear and cool and soothed her parched throat.

She stood, looked up, and began to climb. An ancient track wound through the boulders and stunted trees at the base of the mountains. In many places it seemed to disappear, but she always knew where it was no matter how often it vanished. She would skirt a rock or a thicket of trees and it would be there before her like a thin thread of moon's light.

She followed it up and up until she neared the snow. Yet even though it should have been cold, she was warm. Heat rose off her body and she continued on, leaving tracks in the snow that melted behind her.

Then suddenly she was at the entrance of a cave. There was nothing to suggest the opening, but she knew it was there. She looked at it, feeling as if she had been here once a very long time before.

A pool of water nearby beckoned. Brys filled her hands with water and drank. Then, without thinking, she stepped into the pool and submerged herself until she felt cool. Only then did she return to the cave.

Ducking beneath a huge out thrust rock ledge, she entered the cavern beyond.

The inside was illuminated by some invisible means and Brys could see everything clearly.

The cave was warm and dry with carpets and pillows on the floor. Hangings covered the walls and it felt as if she had arrived home.

Suddenly she was aware she was not alone.

Turning, Brys saw a woman standing on the far side of the cave. She looked as if she had been old for thousands of summers.

"Who are you?" Brys asked.

"I am the Keeper," the woman croaked. "Thank the gods you have arrived. I have not much time left."

"What would you have me do?"

"Return to me as soon as you can," she answered as she inched her way forward. "There are many obstacles and challenges, but you are the Khevira. You must get here quickly. You must get here before I am gone."

She held out her hand and Brys saw she was holding a round medallion. It was covered with strange markings and had a small crystal in the center.

"This will guide you on your journey," she told Brys as she pressed it into her hand. "Wear it always and it will keep you safe."

"But what is your name?" Brys asked.

"I am the Keeper," the woman repeated.

Then she seemed to dissolve in front of Brys' eyes. Brys reached out to take her hand, but the old woman was gone.

Brys backed out of the cave and stood at the mouth looking down at the valley before her. Snow lay in great mounds around her, but the heat seemed to increase. As it did, she began to hear chanting in the distance.

It got louder and louder.

Suddenly she was galloping on the back of a white horse through a thick mist.

The chanting grew louder.

She clutched the medallion in her left hand while her right gripped the snow white mane.

And then she was back in the tent.

Hands held her down. Other hand soothed her face and arms.

Brys looked at them and the last of the mist coalesced into faces.

When they saw she was awake, they helped her rise.

Something cut into her hand and she looked down.

She was still clutching the medallion in her hand.

She heard a gasp.

"Kheran," one of them called.

Esyllt came over, her face wreathed in smiles.

"Look." The women pointed to the medallion in Brys' hand.

All color fled Esyllt's face and her expression changed from smiles to shock.

Puzzled, Brys looked at the medallion and then at the Kheran.

The Kheran came over and lifted Brys' hand to see the medallion more closely.

"It is the Khuriyat Khitan," she said, her voice tinged with awe.

She looked at Brys sharply. "Where did you get this?"

"She said she was the Keeper," Brys said. *Had she done something wrong?*

The other women drew back slightly, but enough for Brys to notice.

"In your spirit journey?" the Kheran asked.

Brys nodded, her throat dry.

The Kheran studied her face. "You must tell me about your experience later. But first, you must be thirsty."

She gestured and one of the women handed Brys a water skin.

The water was cool on Brys' throat and she could have drained the whole skin, but after she had taken but a few sips, they pulled it away.

"Too much is not good," one of the women said. "You may have more in a little while, but you must first eat."

Brys was led back to her place on the circle and she sat on a cushion that had been placed there. Not knowing what else to do, she hung the medallion around her neck. The chain was long and the disk fell between her breasts.

The Kheran stood before them next to the brazier which was now dim, the fire nearly out. The other women lined the tent behind Brys and the other girls.

The Kheran clapped her hands and seven women again carried trays to each of the initiates. The trays held a cup of water and another packet of meat wrapped in grape leaves.

"This will help you complete your journey," the Kheran told them.

Brys at the meat and drank the water. There must have been a restorative in the water, as energy flowed once again through her body.

"Rise," the Kheran commanded.

Brys rose with the help of the other women. Then she and the other girls were led behind the hangings.

There, another brazier was burning and seven tubs full of water waited, the ends pointing at the center of the circle.

Brys stood next to one of the tubs as the Kheran took her place in the center where all the tubs pointed.

"Once again I ask, are you ready to wash away what you once were and become Khutulun?"

"I am," Brys answered when it was her turn.

"Then remove your shifts and wash away the last traces of your old life and be born into the life of Khutulun."

Brys pulled off the now sticky shift and handed it to one of the women. She left the medallion handing around her neck.

The women helped her into the tub. The water was hot and she sank into it gratefully. The women scrubbed her and washed her hair and poured more hot water over her until Brys felt she had never been cleaner.

Finally she was allowed to step out of the tub. Then she was guided to the front of the tub where she was handed new riding pants, sandals and a red vest. Once she had put those on, a red cloak was hung over her shoulders and she was handed a small pile of new clothes.

"I welcome you to kereit Khutulun," the Kheran said, again all smiles. "You will be shown to your new tents and you must rest for this night's ceremonies."

The women led the girls from the tent. But when Brys would have followed, the Kheran touched her arm and had her wait.

"I would speak with you about your spirit journey," she said.

Brys told her what she had seen. She hoped the Kheran would explain it, but the Kheran merely nodded.

"What does it mean?" Brys asked finally.

"I must think upon this," the Kheran said. "Meanwhile, you are tired and you need to rest. We will speak again later."

Then she was gone.

Still dazed, Brys followed a woman to a tent where Idris and five others waited.

Brys embraced Idris, pleased to see her friend. "We are to stay together?"

"I am so pleased," Idris said. "One of our number went to the warriors, so we had a place for you." She turned to the others and made the introductions.

Then she turned back to Brys. "I know you are tired. You must sleep so you can finish the ceremony this evening.

"There is more?" Brys asked, dismayed. She could not imagine what else could possibly happen that would make her more Khutulun than she already was.

Idris grinned. "Indeed. And you must be well rested."

She showed Brys her sleeping mat.

Brys removed her new clothes and sank onto her sleeping mat gratefully. Idris pulled a soft red blanket over her. Then Idris and the others left the tent.

Brys cupped the medallion with her hand and wondered what it meant. Why had everyone been been so shocked when they saw it?

Then sleep claimed her before she could think about it further.

GERAINT

Geraint had worked with the small crystal along side Seren during the previous two days, but had been unable to do or see anything. The crystal had just lain there like a clump of horse dung and he had worried that perhaps he did not have the Talent she thought.

Then on the third day, everything changed.

Seren had gone to perform a healing and had left him alone in the tent. Geraint found it strange that he could feel her presence leave the tent a few short trots after she had gone. But once her presence was gone, he could suddenly feel the presence of his small crystal.

Geraint sat on the cushion in the center of the tent and opened his mind to it. He cupped the crystal in his hand and it began to grow hot.

One moment he was in the tent and then next he was soaring high above the valley. He could see all the tents with a clarity that knifed into him. More, as he soared over individual tents, he could feel swirls of emotions rising up as if they were smoke from a cook fire. Many felt full of joy or excitement, but some were dark and hot.

It was exhilarating and terrifying at the same time.

He felt drawn to a tent across the valley on the other side of the race course. As he drew closer, he felt Seren's presence.

He sensed her looking up and then he felt a push. Suddenly he found himself back in his body in Seren's tent. The crystal around his neck lost its heat and went dim.

Geraint gasped and cried out. The shock of the change was so sudden, it was as if a shirka had been thrust into his heart. The feeling of freedom he had felt while soaring over the valley had been so exquisite that returning to his stunted body left him feeling bereft, as if he had been abruptly yanked off his horse and plunged to the ground.

Geraint made his way to the water skin on shaky legs. He had just taken a gulp of water when Seren thrust open the tent flap.

Her face was ashen as she stared at him.

He could see her throat working as if there was something of great import she needed to say.

Then something in the air changed and the moment fled.

She let the flap close behind her and walked to the center of the tent and put the box with the Great Crystal in its place of honor. Then she turned to look at him.

"We shall have to work on your control now that your Talent has shown itself," she said in a strangly voice. "However, for now we must prepare for tomorrow's ceremony. Once the Tanaiste is over, we will have time to hone your skill. We will discuss your experience later when we have recovered," she added. "We both need a ritual bath and then you will tell me what you saw."

Then she stepped into her private quarters at the back of the tent.

NEIREN

Neiren looked around in nervous anticipation as the matter of the dhavara was finally to be discussed.

Several of the more important Dhervina were present and stood along the edge of the tent. Even Yorath of Kypchak Ulshyn was there. Neiren knew Yorath often did the Great Khagan's bidding and wondered if he was there to report on the decision.

"Are you still going to speak against the boy?" Ofyed asked, his eyes narrow with concern.

Neiren nodded. "If we do not banish him, I fear there will be terrible consequences."

"It is wrong and they will not agree with you." Ofyed paused, then put his hand on Neiren's arm. "I will not support you in this."

"I agree it is wrong for the boy," Neiren said. "But it is right for the Dhervina." He gripped Ofyed's arm. "This is something I have to attempt."

Then his name was called.

Neiren rose and stepped to the middle of the tent to address the Council.

"Neiren of family Darligyn, kereit Malika, Kypchak Kishyn. You wish to speak on the matter of the dhavara who has come of age this summer."

"I do," Neiren said.

"You are not of his kereit."

"I am not."

"Do you know of something against this boy?"

"I do not."

"Have there been complaints against the boy?"

"Yes. But only here at the Tanaiste. And all complaints were of little consequence as the boy was acting as a normal boy."

"Then what is it you wish to speak of?"

Neiren took a moment to gather his thoughts.

"The three complaints I have received were only of a boy acting as a boy who has just come of age. Visiting other kereits, asking questions and speaking to a servant of the family of another Kypchak."

"No unfortunate incidents? Evidence of ostuda caused by him?"

"None," Neiren said. "The boy has proved himself worthy of being deemed Dhervina."

"Then you support his acceptance into the Dhervina."

"I do not."

The room went still.

"You oppose the boy?"

"I do."

Neiren scanned the room, looking at each of the dheren in turn before return his attention to the Great Dheren on the seat of judgment.

"Geraint is a capable boy who has demonstrated good skill in the breeding of horses. He obeys all of our laws and conducts himself as a true Dhervina. If it were not for his unfortunate birth, we would be proud to call him Dhervina. I have also been told by the Guardian for Kypchak Kishyn that the boy has a strong Talent and they have begun his training in the way of the Guardians. So he is an extraordinary boy in many ways."

A buzz filled the tent at the unexpected news. Neiren waited for it to die down before he resumed.

"However." Here Neiren paused and scanned the faces of each of the dheren yet again.

"I believe it is mistake to confirm the boy as Dhervina. I believe he should be banished at the end of the Tanaiste. Should we not do so, I believe there will be terrible consequences."

Out of the corner of his eye he saw Aeron flap his hand in disgust. But Neiren was determined to continue in the hopes that enough of the others would see the sense in what he was saying.

"Even here at the Tanaiste, the boy has been pursued and treated with hostility. I believe that only the strict rules of the Tanaiste have kept him from being abused or killed. Once the Tanaiste has concluded, there will be nothing to stop the boy, and possibly his family, from being destroyed. We would be doing the dhavara and the Dhervina a kindness to banish him. He will never be accepted."

He paused to let his words sink in.

"I also believe that if we do not banish him, the people will lose all respect for the dheren and will take matters into their own hands. And that will lead to anarchy and chaos."

Now he saw most of the other dheren shaking their heads and he knew his cause was lost.

"It is in the interest of all to banish the boy."

There were no questions and Neiren returned to his seat.

The Great Dheren stood. "We will break for the evening meal and to think on what Neiren has said. Let us return here after the meal and make our final decision."

Neiren waited until the others left and only Ofyed remained.

"Did I convince you, at least?" Neiren asked.

"No, my friend." The other man looked around the now empty tent. "The law is clear. The boy deserves to be welcome as Dhervina. The law says he cannot be denied."

"Even if it will lead to destruction?"

"Even if. But I do not believe that will happen."

"If I cannot convince you, then it is unlikely I convinced anyone else."

"I do not think it will be as dire as you imagine."

"I can only hope you are correct," Neiren said. But his heart felt like stone as he followed his friend from the tent.

YORATH

Yorath returned to the Council of Dheren after the evening meal to hear their final decision about the dhavara.

He had heard the inspired words of Dheren Neiren earlier and hoped they would be sufficient to persuade the Council of Dheren to make the correct decision.

But it was clearly not to be. As each dheren was asked, each in turn responded 'yes'. Only Neiren and one other said 'no'.

Yorath marked their names and left the tent in disgust.

When he returned to his tent, the others had already gathered to hear the news.

"Only Neiren of Malika and Goronwy of the Jirgin understood the danger," he told them. "The others all confirmed the dhavara is Dhervina."

"No!" Andras pushed his way to the front. "This cannot be."

"Yet it is so," Yorath said.

He looked at the group of men who shared his concern.

"Spread the word," he said. "Let all know the decision and let them know, too, that Neiren and Goronwy are to be protected."

After the others had left, Andras came up to him.

"Is that all you are going to do?" he demanded.

Yorath wondered if he should tell the boy what had been set in motion, then decided it might be better if Andras knew nothing. He was still young and untried.

"There is little more I can do at the moment," he told the boy. "Tomorrow is the last day of the Tanaiste. Much can happen once the Tanaiste is concluded and we have left the sacred valley."

He saw understanding arise in the boy's eyes.

Andras bowed slightly in respect. "Forgive my rash words, my father-to-be," he said humbly. "I should not have doubted you."

Yorath nodded absently. His mind had already moved on to Rhian. He was as full of rage as an untamed horse and he needed a good ride. Unlike his wife, Rhian could not deny him and he could do as he pleased with her.

He particularly enjoyed catching her unaware and now went in search of her.

Tegan

Tegan finally had to admit defeat. For three sun cycles he had not seen even the slightest movement in the tent below and he wondered if the dhavara had found out what he was up to or if something had happened.

His friends had already quit, tired of watching for the dhavara who never came. Even Kelmon, who he could usually cow into doing whatever he wanted, had walked away.

Now that the Council of Dheren had made their decision, he had hoped that if he helped rid the Dhervina of the dhavara, Yorath might consider letting him ride with his kereit. Tegan was sick of riding in the south with others who had no taste for fighting or the gaining the spoils of battle.

BRYS

When she awoke, it was dark and for a few moments, Brys did not know where she was. Then she saw her red vest and a broad grin nearly split her face.

I really am Khutulun now. It had not been a dream. She dressed and then sat on her sleeping mat wondering what she should do now.

While she waited, Brys examined the medallion, but the carvings on it meant nothing to her and after a time she let it hang. Perhaps the Kheran knew. She thought it unlikely that it would have been given to her if there were not some way to decipher it and obey the old woman's command to reach her as soon as possible.

Then Idris entered and Brys rose to greet her.

"My heart is glad you have arisen already," Idris said. "The sleep after the spirit journey is most deep and it often takes a long time to awaken from it."

"What is to happen next?" Brys asked.

But Idris only shook her head. "You will see," she promised. "You must remove your sandals now. They are not allowed."

Brys slipped them off quickly. "Am I dressed correctly?" she asked.

"Yes."

"What about my ribbons?"

Idris grinned. "They look beautiful in your hair. They are tied well and you look like a Khutulun. You will do well this night."

"When do we go?" Brys asked, anxious to find out what came next.

"You will see." Idris laughed. "And it will be soon now. You must learn patience," she added. "There are many times when we have to wait and patience becomes necessary."

The other women entered the tent now and Brys forgot her impatience as she met each of them again. This time their faces did not run together and she was glad to have the chance to get to know her new sisters.

Brys knew it was time for the final ceremony when a war drum began pounding. The tent flap was thrust open and Brys jumped to her feet.

A second drum joined in and then another and another until it seemed every war drum in the valley had been pressed into service.

Idris took her hand and the others of her new tent crowded around her and led her back through the spiral to the center of the camp.

As she walked, she saw the other initiates also surrounded and on their way to the center.

Now the tent flaps of the other Khutulun were pinned open and the way was lined with the older Khutulun, all barefoot and wearing their red vests.

Brys wondered how they all were to fit within the tent, but when she got to the center, she saw it would not be difficult. The tent was gone and in its place a huge fire was blazing.

The Kheran stood in front of the fire and waited until all the girls stood before her and the space was crammed with all ages of women.

The Kheran raised her arms and the drums abruptly stopped.

"I have before me new Khutulun to welcome to our camp," she shouted. "They have made their pledge. They have eaten the sacred food and drunk the sacred tea. They have stripped away their old lives and returned from the journey through the land of shadows."

She paused and looked at each of the girls in turn. Her eyes seemed to linger on Brys for longer than the others before her gaze moved on.

The Kheran now looked beyond at the rest of the Khutulun.

"They have proven themselves worthy," she shouted. "Do you welcome them to our tents?"

The women roared their approval.

The same seven women from earlier returned again carrying trays. An eighth offered a tray to the Kheran.

The Kheran ate the meat and downed the tea in a single gulp.

Then Brys and the others did the same.

Idris then took one hand and someone else took her other and soon Brys was dancing around the fire.

But after going around the fire only seven times, Brys found herself returned to the center.

Now a path of fire was laid out before her.

Suddenly the Kheran began dancing. She jumped and twirled and twisted every which way and only when her body was slick and shiny with sweat did she dance her way onto the river of fire. She danced to the end and then stood facing the way she had come.

She began clapping.

"It is the Dance of Fire," Idris said. "You must do as the Kheran did."

Brys' head was swimming and she wondered briefly if she had the courage. Then she remembered how the snow in her spirit journey had melted when she stepped through it.

Brys began to dance.

She let her body catch the rhythm of the drums and the pounding in her blood. Suddenly she knew it was time and she danced all the way down the river of fire until she reached bare ground.

The Kheran embraced her tightly. "Now you are truly Khutulun," she said.

And then Brys was whirled away by the others and she danced around the fire as the other girls performed the Dance of Fire.

She danced until the sweat ran into her eyes and the fire turned to ash.

Finally as the moon began its descent behind Khurtagin, she returned to her tent and sank into a long and dreamless sleep.

Geraint

That night, Geraint's dreams were again filled with fire and shouts of anger. It woke him in the time of darkness and for a moment he could barely breathe.

His mouth was filled with the taste of ashes and his body felt as if he had been beaten. Even the muscles in his legs twitched as if he had been running. It took several gallops, but gradually the quiet settled in and he was able to catch his breath.

He caressed the crystal hanging around his neck. Were his nightmares caused by the crystal? Or was he "seeing" something that was to come?

Then the tent flap opened and he saw Seren standing there, her hair tangled and her face drawn.

"Did you dream?" she asked.

"Yes."

SEREN

Seren listened as Geraint described his dreams.

She blessed the summers of training that allowed her to mask her feelings. To have dreams like this so early surely had to be a sign that he was the Khevira. She knew she should inform the other Guardians, but decided to wait. Geraint was *her* find and she wanted to savor the knowledge for a time. Besides, she told herself, it was still much too early.

"Dreams are the price of crystal Talent," she told him. "The crystal magnifies the intensity, but it is important you never remove it, regardless of dreams or anything else. This is an important time for you. You are tuning yourself to the crystal and growing your ability. It is not always easy, but it is necessary."

"So they are nothing more than bad dreams?"

"Nothing more," she assured him. "Now you must sleep. We have much to do in once the sun's light enters the valley."

But as he lay down on his sleeping mat, she wondered. Surely it was too soon to see what was to come? But if he was the Khevira....

Seren turned away from her thoughts. He is too young, she told herself firmly. And while she had also seen glimpses of fire and ash, it could not happen at the Tanaiste.

So what else could they be but bad dreams?

GERAINT

The final day of the Tanaiste found Geraint up long before the sun rose over Khurilar.

Although he was anxious to begin working near the Great Crystal, it was far too early. The Guardian would not awake for some time. Which meant he had to work with his smaller crystal as best he could until she was ready for him to come to her tent.

So far he had enjoyed working with the crystal, but this morning he found it difficult to concentrate. No matter how often he cleared his mind, excitement reared up and before he knew it, he was once again dreaming of what the days ahead would bring.

He had received word after the evening meal that he had been confirmed as full Dhervina and he still had not yet taken in the news. After all the summers of uncertainly and fear, he could now suddenly take his place as if he was an ordinary Dhervina.

The news had kept him awake late into the time of darkness and he suspected it would take many turns of the moon before he truly believed it to be real.

And then there had been the nightmares.

He remembered what Seren had said, but the dreams were so real that they left him unsettled.

After several failed attempts to activate the crystal, he abandoned the effort and made his way to the tent of necessity.

By the time he returned, there was sufficient light to dress and prepare for the summons from the Guardian.

He hoped she would rise early, as well. The exercises she had given him seemed to work better near the Great Crystal.

After the morning meal, Seren explained what would happen.

"On this last day, the Guardians will all stand in the center of the Valley. After the final race, we will fuse the Great Crystals into one. Then we will send the Blessing throughout the entire valley so that all Dhervina will be touched by the energy of the Great Crystal. It not only blesses them, but links us all together."

"It is of great import, then?" Geraint couldn't remember the last Tanaiste very well and wondered if he had been present at the Blessing then. He wanted to ask why the Blessing hadn't made him tall and straight as the other Dhervina. But he said nothing. He suspected neither the Blessing nor even the Great Crystal could alter his appearance.

"It is what has kept us together as a people when so many others have disappeared or been destroyed." Seren explained. "There is a part of us that needs the power of the crystal. Without it, we would quickly wither. Then those who would destroy us would have no difficulty obliterating us. The crystal binds the Dhervina together until the next Tanaiste.

"It is much like what you are doing when you work with the crystal. You are tuning yourself to the crystal. In the same manner, the Dhervina are tuned to the crystal and need that energy to stay Dhervina."

"If anyone goes out among the Duta'ut for a long time, would they die?" Geraint asked.

"They might," Seren said. "Or they could become weak or ill. That is why Guardians in training attend any Dhervina traveling a great distance. She keeps them in harmony until they return."

"Will I be able to travel also when I am older?"

"Possibly," Seren said. "But as you are a special case, we would have to determine that when that time comes."

ANDRAS

While Andras respected his father-to-be, he was not content to wait until after the Tanaiste to see the dhavara dealt with. Especially since he would be traveling north with his new family and the dhavara would return to the south. If something *was* done, he might never even hear about it. He certainly would not see it and that was something he dearly desired.

He considered some of the things he had set in motion and thought of yet another thing he could do to ensure the dhavara was removed.

After the morning meal, Andras returned to the Talfryn camp. He had heard that the Talfryn rider he had spoke with at the beginning of the Tanaiste was to ride in the final race.

Andras had seen him ride. Although he had good tricks, he didn't have as much control as he needed. One small mishap and he would go flying.

It didn't take him long to find the Talfryn rider. Predictably he was walking the horse up and down the center of the racecourse. It let everyone see the horse before the race in order to encourage wagers.

When the rider paused briefly, Andras waved him over.

The Talfryn rider looked down on him with a puzzled look on his face.

"Have we spoken?" he asked.

"At the beginning of the Tanaiste," Andras reminded him. "I helped you up after the dhavara caused you to fall."

"Ahh," the rider said, but he still looked unsure.

Andras remembered the rider had been drunk and so probably barely remembered. It was good he had thought to return.

"I have heard that the dhavara will be watching you from near the Guardian's tent," Andras told him.

"What is that to me?" the rider asked indifferently. "All the Dhervina will be watching." He pulled on the reins and started turning the horse. Andras saw his hopes about to ride away.

"I have heard he placed a curse on your success," Andras said quickly. "I only wanted to warn you."

The Talfryn looked down at Andras, suspicion riding on his face.

"Why would he do this?"

Andras shrugged. "You frightened him. And he has a friend riding against you."

"And why do you tell me this? I do not know you."

"I thought you should know," Andras replied, trying to sound as if it was not important to him. "You are easily the best rider and the dhavara should not be allowed to cause you to lose the race. Now, perhaps you will be prepared and keep his curse from making you fall."

"Fall?" The Talfryn rider laughed. "I never fall. Watch the race today and see. This curse you mention? It is not strong enough to cause me to fall."

With that, he dug his heels into the horse and they trotted back up the raceway.

Andras watched him go, hoping his words had created enough doubt to weigh on the rider's mind.

Then he returned to his tent to prepare for the final race. He didn't know what else he could do. But if nothing happened at the race, then whatever Yorath had planned would have to suffice.

TALFRYN RIDER

All the other races during the Tanaiste led up to this last race. And all saved the most daring for this race, all for the chance to win glory and honor at the final race of the Tanaiste. And all the riders kept their intentions for this final race well guarded.

Every Dhervina in the valley would be in attendance. Better yet, the Great Khagan himself would be riding. He had won at the last three Tanaistes and was considered impossible to beat despite his advancing age. The chance to defeat the Great Khagan at this Tanaiste was like a burr under Maxon's skin. It had gnawed at him ever since the last Tanaiste and he had been determined to find a way to win.

It wasn't enough to beat him to the finish line. He would have to do something daring during the ride to guarantee the win.

Maxon came from a lowly tent in a lowly kereit. He had dreamed of nothing more than the chance to ride with a better kereit. Perhaps even the kereit of the Great Khagan himself would be open to him if he won this race.

In all the races of the Tanaiste, Maxon had proven he was the best rider of the Talfryn. Even so, he knew the other riders had withheld their best tricks for this race. He only hoped that none of them had come up with something as daring as what he would attempt for this final race.

Maxon had watched every race for the past seven summers and had never seen anyone ride without a bridle. They had crouched on the backs of their horses and had even ridden underneath. But always it was with a bridle.

A bridle was the only sure way to control the horse. Going without was very difficult and extremely risky.

He had practiced riding with no bridle or saddle for nearly five summers and had beaten everyone from his kereit for the past two. More importantly, he had not fallen or lost control of his horse for the past two summers.

Now he wove the red and gold ribbons of kereit Talfryn into the mane of his horse thinking how fine they would look as he thundered to victory.

The memory of the dhavara and his stumble darkened his thoughts briefly. He had nearly forgotten his encounter with the dhavara until the one called Andras of Malika had come to warn him again. The talk in the kereit the previous evening had all been about the dhavara, but Maxon had given it little heed. *What did he care?* It was not as if it had anything to do with him.

But now he wondered. Had the dhavara truly cursed his ride?

Maxon shook his head, the ribbons in his hair whipping in the fine breeze.

He was the best rider in the valley. No curse from a small dhavara could cost him the race. He stroked the neck of his horse.

"We will out ride them all," he promised. "All the horses will be envious and you will mount all the mares of your choosing."

GERAINT

Geraint had been too young at the previous Tanaiste to understand or be aware of anything but the excitement, colors and horses. But this time, he was a part of it and was discovering what the Guardians had to do, especially this last day. They had many more duties than he could have imagined. And all the preparations took time. Especially on this last day of the Tanaiste.

And then, when the preparations were complete, they had to stop for the mid-day meal. Although Geraint was famished by that time, he was anxious to get to the raceway and see the final race. He had missed all the races thus far, so this would be his only chance. As it was the biggest race of the festival, he could barely wait.

"You must eat," Seren told him when she saw he wanted nothing more than to depart. "They will not begin without us and you must be strong for the ceremony."

Geraint had no choice but to spend an inordinate amount of time at the meal, but chafed at the delay.

Finally, though, they finished and Geraint followed Seren and the two handmaidens to where they would watch the final race of the Tanaiste. Once that was over, the Guardians would perform the Blessing in the heart of the valley. It was held at the exact center and Seren had told him that it was where the Great Crystal had been found by the first Guardian.

This final race was no ordinary race. The winner of this race would not only win the glory of being the best rider of the Dhervina, he would be given the chance to change to a better kereit and make a much more advantageous alliance than would have been possible before.

The riders in this race had beaten all the others until only these eight were left. This race would determine who was the fastest and most daring of the Dhervina. Geraint had been excited to discover that Yurki of Geraint's own kereit was one of those who would compete in the final race. Better yet, he was riding the horse Geraint had helped breed, and had defeated the Jirgin rider who had been a favorite.

And of those riders, only the Talfryn rider and the Great Khagan posed any real competition from what Geraint had heard thus far. So Yurki had a good chance of winning. It was doubly exciting because their kereit had never won the final race and was small and poor. Geraint hoped his friend would do well. Their kereit would be celebrating and telling the story for many summers.

Rhian

Yorath had kept Rhian close ever since he had caught her returning late. Not only had he ridden her as often as he had when he first took her captive, but he had insisted she come to the Tanaiste's final races so he could ride her as soon as the race was over.

She had hoped to use the occasion to move the last of her supplies, but at least they were ready. All she had to do was find an excuse to be away from his presence long enough not to excite his suspicions.

She was nearly certain he had no idea she planned to escape. She suspected he thought she was riding with someone else. How else to explain his renewed desire to mount her so frequently. She hoped he would continue to believe that. If he knew the truth, he would take his rage out on her in a much less subtle manner. Yorath was not one for intrigue or taking the long trail.

Even so, it was nearly as bad as when she had first been taken in the Dhervina raid on her homeland. Then he had had a guard with her at all times when he was not riding her. At least this time there was no guard. Unfortunately, he was suspicious by nature and she would have to be extremely cautious.

"There."

Rhian saw the new son-to-be pointing further up the valley. She craned her head to see what he was pointing to. At first, the crowd was so thick she could see nothing.

Then it parted briefly and she saw the tall imposing figure of a Guardian. She wondered why Yorath was so upset. Then she caught a glimpse of the dhavara standing next to her.

Rhian's hand rose to cover her mouth in surprised. *What was he doing there?* Then she though of how angry Yorath had been after the boy's visit.

She looked over at Yorath. His jaw was clenched and his eyes were narrow with rage.

There will be trouble, she thought.

Rhian immediately abandoned her plan to ask Geraint for assistance. He would be lucky to get out of the valley alive. She would be wise to be as far from him as possible.

Then she saw a glimmer of hope. If there was trouble, she might be able to use that to make her escape.

GERAINT

As instructed, Geraint stood next to Pryderi and the other assistants behind the four Guardians. He looked around for Owena to see if she wanted to stand with Pryderi, but she was at the far end busily chatting with the other woman clustered behind Myared, the Guardian of the North.

Geraint caught himself starting to bounce up and down as the riders took their places at the far end of the valley. He supposed he should act in a more dignified manner now that he was training with a Guardian and he tried to keep his excitement in check. But it wasn't easy.

He tried to concentrate on what was to happen. They would ride the length of the valley three times before the finish at the north end. The race would test not only the riders' ability, but the ability and stamina of the horses.

He thought about Yurki's horse and knew it had the stamina. Geraint knew the competition would be stiff and hoped Yurki was up to the difficult trick he intended as he raced down the last lap.

It was late in the day and he knew everyone must be tired on this last day of the Tanaiste. But everyone had dressed in their finery and had come to see the race. Excitement made the very air vibrate as the Dhervina placed wagers and argued about who would take the glory. It was especially exciting since the Great Khagan himself was competing.

Suddenly it was as if he was in a dark tent. There was screaming and ripples of anger washed over him. Geraint was more terrified than he had ever been as blood spilled all around him.

Then, just as quickly, he was back in the light of the sun, waiting for the race to begin.

"No," he whispered. He was about to tell Seren and get her to stop the race when Pryderi put her hand on his shoulder.

He looked up.

She put her hand to her lips and shook her head.

Feeling as if time had stopped, he turned his head slowly, straining to see the horses. There had to be time.

Geraint didn't hear the crack of the whip, but he saw the horses begin their mad gallop down the center of the valley and he put his hand to his mouth to keep his dismay from leaping out.

Talfryn Rider

Maxon felt the horse surge under him almost at the same stride the whip cracked. He tightened his hands on the horse's mane and bent low, keeping his head near the straining neck.

The first two passes around the valley were about speed. This was where the horses would prove their stamina.

Maxon had trained his horse for endurance and now the training showed its worth. His horse easily moved to the front by the end of the first pass. By the second, they were ahead of the others by at least the length of a horse. But Maxon didn't dare look back. He was too concerned about setting up the third pass.

The third pass was not only about stamina, but also the rider's daring.

Maxon would have to slow slightly for this next pass and wanted to get as far ahead as possible. As they made the turn and began the final pass, Maxon carefully pulled his feet up under him and rose to a crouch on the back of his horse, his hand still holding his horse's mane.

The horse next to him thundered closer.

Then, as they neared the center of the valley where most of the Dhervina watched, he rose to his feet, his arms stretched out to the sides.

He turned his head to see the crowd, knowing his kereit would be cheering for him.

But as he did so, his gaze landed on the dhavara.

Maxon started.

Just a small twitch.

But enough.

His horse swerved and then Maxon felt a huge thump as he collided with the horse next to him.

And then he was flying.

The ground rose up to greet him. He had instinctively curled himself into a ball so he would roll, but he hit hard and tumbled more than rolled.

Unable to move at first, he lay on the raceway.

The crowd which had been wildly cheering was now silent.

The he heard the screams of the horses and he turned his head. Several horses lay in a jumble and were screaming.

Including his own.

Although every part of his body screamed in pain, Maxon crawled to his horse.

He didn't need to run his hands over the horse to see the damage. A front leg was twisted and a broken bone jutted out.

Tears streaming down his face, he drew his shirka and cut its throat.

He wanted to rest his head on the best horse he had ever had, but he could still hear another horse screaming.

He looked over.

Horrified, he saw the Great Khagan lying still just beyond his horse which continued screaming even as it tried to rise.

Mercifully, someone came running and cut the horse's throat.

Now there was no sound at all.

One of the Guardians ran out and knelt by the Great Khagan.

"He lives!" she shouted.

Maxon heard cheers but noticed that the Great Khagan did not rise.

He turned his head again and saw once again the face of the dhavara.

Rising unsteadily to his feet, he raised his arm and pointed.

"He cursed me!"

RHIAN

Even though Rhian hated the Dhervina riders with all her heart, the sound of the thundering hooves as the horses raced still entranced her. They rode so hard and the horses were beautiful with their ribbons streaming as they ran.

For a brief moment, it was a glorious sight. The Talfryn rider standing on the back of his horse, arms outstretched and ribbons streaming. The Great Khagan twirling around the middle of his horse, his head perilously close to the pounding hooves.

Then, in an instant, everything changed as the horses collided.

She saw the Talfryn rider fly through the air and roll. But the Great Khagan, who had curled under his horse's belly and was just beginning to come up the other side, was crushed as his horse fell heavily.

The screaming of the horses was horrible and she covered her ears. She could not bear to listen.

The boy who had caused the accident cut his horse's throat. Then another cut the throat of the Great Khagan's horse and it was mercifully quiet again.

She had just taken her hands from her ears when the Talfryn rider stretched out his arm and pointed.

All eyes followed his outstretched hand to the shocked face of the dhavara.

"He cursed me," the Talfryn rider screamed.

Brys

Although all around her were cheering the riders, Brys knew something was wrong. She could not have said what it was or put a bridle on it. But her heart felt the chill of it.

She had caught a glimpse of her brother when the Guardians arrived. He looked happy and she was pleased that all seemed to be going well for him at last. Idris and the other Khutulun from her tent surrounded her and looked as excited as she should have been.

Even so, the heaviness remained.

Unable to bear the weight, Brys eased her way through the crowd. If something went wrong, she wanted to be ready to get Geraint's horse. It had been her promise to him and she knew he would be relying on her to meet him at the cave.

Although her first responsibility belonged to the Khutulun now, she would only have to leave the horse and then could return quickly to the Khutulun.

But the crowd was densely packed and she was still trapped within when she heard the collective gasp and knew that something terrible had happened.

And she was still trapped when she heard the terrible words.

"He cursed me."

Now Brys began clawing her way through, desperate to get free.

But the crowd surged in the other direction. No matter how she fought to go the other way, she was inexorably drawn to the center of the valley.

Geraint

"He cursed me!"

Geraint plunged into the crowd before anyone could react. He quickly found a tent, ducked under the tent wall and scurried inside. He knew he had little time to find a safe way out.

He thought about the cave.

Could he make it?

He had to get out of the valley before the Dhervina knew he had gone.

Geraint lifted the far edge of the tent and peered out.

Too open.

He scurried to the side. The shadow of the next tent would cover his exit. Geraint bent low and sidled along the side of the tent.

He thought about taking the edge of the encampment, but rejected the idea immediately. He would be in the open and easily spotted. They would expect him to go that way or even go to his family's tent. He would have to stay as far away from both as possible.

They would never expect him to stay in the encampment.

Rhian

Yorath bellowed and began pushing through the crowd. Rhian followed for a time, hoping to get through the crowd before they crushed her. But Yorath was forcing his way through so furiously that the crowd simply reformed behind him and soon Rhian was left behind to make her own way through.

The force of the bodies around her made it difficult to break free, but she kept moving to the side and finally made it to the edge of the crowd where she was able to slip through an opening.

She headed directly for the mountains and breathed a sigh of relief when she saw the way was deserted. She ran the length of the encampment until she reached Yorath's tent. It took but a moment to snatch up the last of her things. Then she hurried to where the horses were milling about anxiously. She saddled two of them, her hands shaking so badly she had trouble fastening the girths. But they were finally ready and she led them down the valley as quickly as she could.

Rhian could hear shouting and screams from further up the valley. That poor boy, she thought. She increased her pace. She had to be out of the valley before the violence moved to this end and engulfed her.

Rhian found herself muttering the prayers of her childhood as she went. "Be with me, oh great one. Guide me and protect me and I will praise you for all time." She thought she had forgotten the words of her people since being taken by Yorath's marauders. But the words came back to her easily now and helped her keep panic at bay.

Brys

Realizing she was making no headway, Brys turned and joined the crowd, but moved sideways. Now it was easier to make progress and she finally got to the edge and broke through.

Remembering Geraint telling her about the route down the side of the valley, Brys ran south, skirting the edge of the encampment until she reached their horses.

She thanked the Great Horse they had been prepared. She quickly saddled Geraint's horse, then lashed the extra supplies and his ladder to the saddle.

She began leading the horse away, but stopped when she saw an approaching figure. While she needed to hurry, the last thing she wanted to do was lead someone to their hiding place.

It took a moment before she recognized Geraint's friend, Rhian. Her head was covered, hiding the hair of fire. But the limp gave her away.

Rhian stopped when she saw Brys and her hand went to her mouth in fear.

The two women stared at each other for a long stride.

Then Brys realized they were wasting time.

"You are Geraint's friend, Rhian of Mentos," Brys said. "We spoke three sun cycles ago. I am his sister."

The other woman nodded, her body relaxing slightly.

"You are escaping?" Brys asked even though she already knew the answer.

Rhian nodded and looked back up the valley as if looking for pursuers.

"I will not stop you," Brys said. "You are wise to leave now. Yorath will not miss you until it is much too late." She took a deep breath, hoping her trust was well placed. "We have a secret cave where you can hide until all the Dhervina have left the valley."

Rhian's eyes brightened. "You would do this for me?"

"All I ask is that you bring this horse there for Geraint," Brys said. "If he can escape the trouble, he will go to that cave. There are supplies there for him so he will not be a burden to you."

"I am honored you would trust me," Rhian said. "I will watch for your brother and do what I can to assist him."

Brys described how to find the cave and then handed Rhian the reins to the horse. "I give you my gratitude for your assistance this day, Rhian of Mentos," she said. "Should you ever need assistance, I will be honored to come to your aid."

The shouting began to get louder and Brys realized the crowd was getting closer. They must not have caught Geraint yet.

"Hurry," she said. "You must get out of the valley quickly before they see you."

"What about you?"

"I must see to our parents," Brys said. "Now go."

Rhian nodded and clicked at the horses to get them moving.

Tegan

The sun had moved nearly to the tip of Khurtagin and still the dhavara had not been captured.

Tegan pried himself free of the crowd and scratched his head.

The dhavara was small. What if he had escaped back to his tent already?

While it was unlikely, Tegan hurried south. He was having so little luck here, it was worth a try.

When he reached the dhavara's tent, he saw the flap was closed. He slipped up to the side and put his head against the tent. He listened long enough to hear two voices. One male and one female. It had to be the dhavara and his sister.

He looked around, but no one else was there. Everyone was still in the center of the valley.

Yorath of Besut had told Tegan to find him if he found the dhavara. He was an important warrior and Tegan had visions of riding with Yorath as he hurried back to the center of the valley.

BRYS

Brys waited long enough to make sure Rhian was well away, then started back to her tent. She had to make sure her parents had not returned from their visit to kereit Buriyat.

But as she drew nearer the tent, she saw that the flap was closed which meant they had returned early.

She had to warn them. There was no telling what would happen when the mob reached this end of the valley. It was the Tanaiste, so there should be no trouble, but she had never seen an angry crowd such as this. But then there had never been a serious accident at the races.

She knew it was not his fault, but no one else was likely to believe that in the heat of the moment.

But as Brys ran towards the tent, she was grabbed from behind and a hand covered her mouth to prevent her from calling out.

Then she was dragged into a tent.

"Shhh," her captor said. "Don't say anything. They'll be here any moment."

Brush stopped struggling as she recognized Andras' voice.

"Will you give me your pledge not to shout?" he asked.

Brys nodded and he took his hand away from her mouth, but kept his grip on her arm. She was surprised at how much stronger he was than he appeared.

"I must save my family," she said as she tried to pull away.

His grip tightened. "You cannot."

"They do not know what has happened," she said urgently. "They will be in danger."

He looked away. "There is little you can do now."

She looked at him and realized that he had done something to bring this about.

"What have you done?" she demanded.

"I did it for you," he said. "Someone had to stop him."

She would think about this later. Right now she had to get to her parents. "I can get them out of the tent. Out of the valley."

"It's too late."

Now Brys could hear the roar of the crowd as it neared. It was like the sound they made at the races, but lower and uglier.

She struggled to get free, but he held on tight, wrapping both arms around her to hold her fast.

"I would have had time," Brys screamed.

"I wanted to keep you safe," he told her. "I could not live if they killed you. You should have been mine."

"I am Khutulun. Let me go."

"I will release you when they have gone," he promised.

All Brys could hear now were the shouts and screams outside.

She twisted suddenly and punched him squarely in the nose. His grip loosened and she follow up with a kick to his leg.

Suddenly she was free and she made a dash for the tent flap. As she ducked outside, she was brought to a halt by the crowd that surged around her family's tent.

Geraint must be in there.

She had hoped he had made it out of the valley, but now it seemed he had been caught when he returned to their tent. *And what of their parents?*

She clawed her way into the crowd. A stone inexpertly thrown caught the side of her head and she staggered.

Suddenly she was again caught from behind. Before she could cry out, Andras' hand covered her mouth and he dragged her back into the tent.

This time he struck her face, knocking her down.

Then he was straddling her, pinning her arms to the ground.

"Is this what you want?" he shouted. He began tearing at her clothes.

"No." Brys tried to fight back, but then he began punching her.

She heard an awful crunching sound and felt a terrible pain in her face. Dazed, she could feel only pain as he pummeled her until everything went black.

RHIAN

Once in the pass out of the valley, Rhian spared a moment to look back, but could see nothing. Thick dust swirled about the Dhervina encampment. She had feared to see pursuers emerging, but thankfully saw only dust. While she was not yet truly safe, it gave her a sliver of hope that she might truly escape.

Adding to her good fortune, she saw her supplies were still behind the jumble of rocks and she heaved a sigh of relief.

Soon she had loaded everything onto the horses. She walked as quickly as possible through the pass, looking for the signs Geraint's sister had told her about, once again blessing the chance meeting.

She hoped the boy was able to make it. But if he did not, at least she would be able to escape undetected. Better yet, she could stay there until she was certain the Dhervina had dispersed. After a few days, it would be safe to continue her journey to the south and find a land far away from the Dhervina.

She realized now that had it not been for Brys, she might well have been overtaken in the pass by the Dhervina. Then it would have been much harder to appear as if she belonged with them. Someone would have likely remembered her and send word to Yorath.

Finally she spied the three enormous boulders Brys had told her to look for. She led the horses around to the back and saw the faint whisper of a path leading further in. She followed it until she reached a clearing with a small pond.

From there it was a short climb to the cliff.

Rhian tethered the horses carefully before inspecting the cave. There was little forage for them up here, so she would have to gather some from further down. At least she would be able to do so without being discovered.

The mouth of the cave was nearly invisible as Brys had warned. But Rhian pushed the bushes aside until she saw it.

The entrance was low, but once inside, she was pleased to see the cave was quite large. Better, it was dry and would be a comfortable place to hide.

Rhian returned to the horses and carried all the supplies into the cave. There was always the chance someone might stumble upon the horses, but with nothing on their backs, they would likely not search for the owners.

Once that was done, she rolled her sleeping mat out in the depth of the shadows on the far side of the cave and lay down. She knew she would not sleep, but it felt good to let her body rest after the chaos and repeated assaults by Yorath of the past few sun cycles.

GERAINT

Geraint slipped from shadow to tent and back to shadow until he had crossed most of the valley. He knew he was near the southern end only when he caught sight of the green and black banners of kereit Adargin. They had set up camp just inside the southern edge of the valley. He had passed their tents on the way in on the first day.

He thought sadly of his horse and special saddle and wondered what would happen to them. They had always thought trouble would come when they were near the tent and there would be time for Brys to reach his horse. But she was likely with the Khutulun and wouldn't know about the accident at the races or the accusations by the Talfryn rider.

He would have to trust that Brys would discover what would happen and meet him at the cave. She had repeatedly told him, 'Get to the cave and don't look back. I will meet you there.' So that is what he would do. He would figure out the rest later. It might be difficult, but at least he would survive to do so.

He stopped briefly as he reached the edge of the encampment. The pass lay directly in front of him. The sun sent long shadows through the valley, but there was still a great deal of light so there was little protection once he left this last tent.

He listened, but the shouting still seemed to come from further up the valley. He peered out. Nothing moved except the horses tethered nearby.

Geraint spied a blanket the color of dried grass and slipped it over his head so he was entirely covered except for a small opening to see through. While no one might be nearby, the Dhervina had sharp eyes. If someone looked in this direction and saw movement, they would come to investigate.

Even so, he had to get out of the valley before they realized he had slipped away. Once they figured out that he was no longer in the center of the valley, they would start looking for him at this end.

Taking a deep breath, he moved slowly out of the tent and entered the pass. He made sure to hold the blanket up high enough to keep it from dragging on the ground and give his path away. Every time he saw a large enough rock, he stepped behind it and listened for pursuit. But each time there was nothing but distant shouts and Geraint kept going until the pass curved slightly and he knew he was out of view. Only then did he hurry as fast as he could towards the cave.

SEREN

By the time Seren reached her tent, she was dirty and disheveled and felt as if she had just walked through a sandstorm. Even being a Guardian had not protected her from the frenzy of a mob intent on finding and killing the dhavara.

She knew she could have used her power to push them away, but that was to be done only in the most dire of needs. This had not been one of those times as the anger was not directed at her. So she had pushed through the crowd like any other Dhervina until she could reach the haven of her tent.

Seren half expected Geraint would come here after the accident, but the tent was deserted when she arrived. She was fairly sure she would have heard if he had been captured, so that must mean he was still alive and in hiding.

If he were to come to the tent and ask for her protection, she wasn't sure now what she would do. She knew the accident had not been his doing, but the Talfryn rider's accusation had been heard by too many to make clearing him of blame an easy matter. She would have to fight off a good portion of the Dhervina and the casualties would be terrible. Worse, she feared the amount of blood shed would render the valley contaminated beyond repair.

Was the life of one dhavara worth risking all of that?

And if he truly was the Khevira?

Seren shuddered and hoped Geraint would not seek shelter with her. This was a decision she did not want to make.

Then she wondered how she had misread the signs.

It seemed so obvious now. All the screams, blood, fire and ash were as if straight from her visions.

How could she have seen them as anything but the nightmare it had become?

Pryderi, who had stayed as close to her as a burr on a saddle blanket, brought her a basin of water to clean herself.

"I will be fine," Seren told Pryderi as she took the basin. "Take care of yourself and then I will decide what to do next.

Once Seren was clean again, she dressed in plain black pants and tunic with the white vest.

She opened the box containing the great crystal of Kypchak Kishyn and stared into it, asking what she should do. The answer she received stunned her. She asked again in case she had misunderstood, but the answer came back clearly.

There was no mistake.

She swallowed hard and closed the lid of the box.

She plucked a crystal from her katra manara, wrapped a copper wire around it and then fastened it around her throat.

When everything was prepared, she made her way to Geraint's tent, Pryderi close behind. Her Khutulun guards had arrived while she was preparing and now flanked her, protecting her from the worst of the crowd's pushing.

When she arrived at Geraint's tent, Seren hoped the boy was not there. But it was clear from the movements inside the tent that someone was inside and was struggling to get out.

In the traditional manner, the tent flap had been sewn shut before the stoning began. This time, the Dhervina were also beating the tent with whatever clubs or other objects they had grabbed on the way. Several were using long tent pegs and Seren saw one woman beating the tent with a stick used to get dust out of carpets.

"Guardian." Pryderi tugged at her sleeve. "You must stop them."

Seren stared at Pryderi. Every part of her wanted to intervene, but it was as if she was bound and had a hand over her mouth. The voice of the crystal came back to her clearly.

She shook her head. "There is nothing I can do. If it is so easy to kill him, then he is not the Khevira."

When all movement inside the tent ceased, Seren felt the tears stream down her face as the Dhervina put their torches to the tent. Her heart felt as if it had been filled with lead as she watched the tent and her dreams go up in flames.

"If he was the Khevira, then we have destroyed ourselves," she said.

Seren turned and walked away. If she stayed, it would only condone what had happened here.

GERAINT

Geraint's legs were shaking by the time he reached the cave. Anxious to reach the safety of the cave, he had made the climb with few stops. He clambered over the last slope and stopped in amazement, pain and exhaustion forgotten. He rubbed his eyes to make sure he was not imagining it.

His horse and two others were grazing placidly just outside the cave.

Geraint dropped the blanket and stumbled into the cave, but the woman waiting there was not Brys.

"Rhian?"

"Geraint of Halaka," she said. "My heart is truly glad to see you arrive here safely."

"How did you find this place?" He still could not take it in.

"Your sister," she said. "She saw me escaping and told me of this place. She asked me to bring your horse."

"Why did she not come?"

"She went back for your parents."

Geraint's legs finally failed him and he collapsed onto the cave floor.

"She wasn't supposed to do that," was all he could think to say. The mob had sounded so terrible. What if they recognized her as his sister? They might harm her if they could not find him.

Rhian knelt next to him. "She will come."

Geraint felt hollow. "No."

"You do not know that," she said firmly. "We will wait. She said she would come as soon as she could."

"They spoke truly," Geraint said. "I *am* ostuda."

"You are not. This is *their* doing. Not yours." Rhian took his hand. "You did not cause them to hate you or fear you. You did nothing. They are superstitious and chose to believe you bring ostuda. But it is *them*. They are the ones with ayna'al living in their hearts."

"But now I will survive and my family may not." He felt tears sliding down his face and wiped them away angrily. Tears would not help and tears would not keep them safe.

"We do not know what is happening and there is nothing you can do in any case," Rhian said as she got to her feet. "We should eat."

He shook his head. "I couldn't." The thought of eating while his family was in danger repelled him.

"We need to be strong now. Refusing to eat will make you weak. I have some bread and honey." She pulled a small packet out of a basket. "I could not take much before I left, but this will do us both good."

She handed him a small piece of bread with a dab of honey.

"It will make you feel better. Eat."

He ate and he did feel better.

"You see?" Rhian brought him a water skin.

He drank greedily, only then realizing how thirsty he had become in escaping the valley.

"Now we will wait until they have all gone."

Geraint nodded and closed his eyes, wondering how long they would need to hide in the cave.

He must have slept, because when he opened his eyes, all the light in the cave was gone. He could only see the entrance to the cave because of the silvery light outside.

"Brys?" he called out. "Are you here?"

Rhian's disembodied voice came out of the darkness.

"She has not yet arrived."

Geraint stood and brushed himself off. "I am going to look."

"We should stay here."

"There is a place where we can see, but they cannot see us," he told her.

Geraint crept out of the cave and, staying tight to the side of the mountain, made his way to the overlook.

He had to know what was going on.

The valley seemed lit by thousands of torches that moved this way and that. It looked as if several tents were on fire. He heard shouts followed by screams and wondered who they were taking their rage out on since he was no longer there.

He felt a hand on his shoulder.

"They still look for you." She draped a blanket over him.

He shivered, the blanket doing little to warm the ice that chilled his blood.

"Do you think they will search the hills?" she asked.

"I wish I knew. If they don't find me in the valley, they may believe I vanished suddenly like a demon."

"You are too small to be a demon," she said. "And you have no tail."

He smiled slightly. It was true that the Dhervina believed their demons to be seven paces tall with horns and a tail.

"We found this place by chance," he told her. "If they decide to search these hills, they could easily discover this place, as well. Or they may not be clear headed enough to scour the mountains to find a place where a dhavara might hide." He shrugged. "I think it safe enough. In any event, there is nowhere else to go."

They returned to the cave.

Geraint intended to keep watch. He doubted he would be able to sleep as the events of this disastrous day kept playing over and over in his mind.

But he was exhausted and sleep finally overtook him.

SEREN

It was not until she returned to her tent that Seren remembered that the Blessing had not been done. She was about to send Pryderi to the other Guardians, then stopped.

There will be no Blessing this summer.

She put her hand to her mouth in shock, but the message had been clear.

This truly was a day of ayna'al. That old dheren had had the right of it after all.

She turned to Pryderi. "We must leave as soon as possible. The sacred peace has been broken and we cannot stay. Tell our Khutulun to begin packing, then gather your own things. We will be leaving as soon as possible. I will begin packing while you are doing that."

"What about Owena?"

"She has gone to serve Guardian Wynne. She will not return." She saw Pryderi's face. "It doesn't matter. Now go. We must leave this place quickly."

To her credit, Pryderi didn't hesitate. She hurried off to do her errand and Seren began packing quickly without regard to what went in which basket. They could sort everything out later.

Even without opening the box that held the large crystal, Seren could feel malign energy fill the valley. She only hoped Pryderi and the Khutulun worked quickly so they could leave before the last of the sun's light left the valley.

ANDRAS

Sanity returned once his rage wore itself out. Only then did Andras realize that Brys lay on the tent floor, her face unrecognizable and her arms and legs lying every which way.

"Brys?"

She did not move and he realized he had killed her.

Outside, the shouting and screaming continued, mirroring his own dismay at what he had done. He had only meant to protect her, not be the one who caused her death.

Then he realized that if anyone discovered he had killed another Dhervina, especially a blameless Khutulun, they would do the same to him as they had done to the dhavara. He had to get her body out of the tent before his parents returned. The crowd was likely keeping them away, but it would tire once the tent was burning and there was nothing more for them to take their anger out on. Then his parents and servants would return quickly.

Andras rolled Brys into her red cloak, then hurried to look out the flap. The crowd was yelling curses at the now burning tent. Their backs were all to him and Andras knew he had a chance to get her out unseen.

Once he was sure the way was clear, he dragged the body out of the back of his tent. She was heavier than he had expected and he was sweating profusely by the time he was able to get far enough away so that no one would connect him with her death. He found a place to leave her behind some rocks that lay at the foot of the mountain and made sure the red cloak was securely wrapped around her.

If someone found her, they would think it happened during the riot or perhaps when one of the rocks fell.

He took one last look, grateful that all he could see now was the red cloak, then hurried away.

It wasn't his fault, he told himself. He had tried to save her even though she had rejected him. But she hadn't wanted him to do even that. It was her own doing.

SEREN

As Seren helped load the horses, she noted many others doing the same. So not all the Dhervina had gone crazy, after all.

She was also grateful that the Great Khagan had suffered no more than a broken arm and a stunning to the head. Guardian Myared had survived the Tanaiste after all and had sent word that the Great Khagan would live, so that particular concern had gone. Myared was keeping him asleep while his head healed, so there was no one to stop the Dhervina rampaging the valley.

When the everything was loaded, Seren and the others mounted and rode slowly through the valley, snaking their way through the tents and gatherings until they reached the far side of the valley. It would be easier to leave the valley this way rather than through the center as was her custom.

They rode past Geraint's still burning tent. It was more ash than flames now, but she still averted her eyes as they passed. She did not want to think about what had happened or what the future might now hold.

They were nearly out of the valley when Seren saw a glimpse of red off to her left as they passed a large boulder.

She pulled back on the reins to halt the horse and raised her hand. "Stop!"

She looked at her head Khutulun riding by her side and pointed.

The Khutulun sucked in her breath sharply and dismounted. She went around the boulder and cried out a brief hoof beat later.

"I need assistance," she shouted.

The other Khutulun dismounted and hurried over.

Her head Khutulun returned a hoof beat later. "Our sister is badly injured. We must return her to kereit Khutulun so she may be healed. One will stay with you until we return."

Seren dipped her head in acknowledgment. "We will wait for you in the mouth of the pass," she said. "You must hurry. It is not good to remain here after the sun's light has left the valley."

"I understand."

The Khutulun carefully loaded the injured woman onto their horses and rode back into the valley.

Seren clicked her tongue getting her horse moving again. The others followed, but as they rode, Seren noticed Pryderi looking back every so often.

"What is it you are looking for?" she asked.

"I worry they may not be able to return to us, Guardian," Pryderi said. "The Dhervina have gone mad."

Seren smiled. Pryderi had very little knowledge of the power of the Khutulun.

"They will return," she assured her. "They are Khutulun."

Seren didn't let them stop until they were well into the pass and beyond the ayna'al filling the valley.

She turned to face the remains of the Tanaiste and cupped the crystal in her hand. Concentrating, she sent the energy out to add a layer of protection to the Khutulun that would protect them until they all were safely out of the valley.

As she concentrated, she could feel the other Guardians adding their power and knew that whatever else transpired, at least the Guardians, the crystals, and the Khutulun would continue.

NEIREN

Neiren had packed up his tent shortly after the crowd began searching for the dhavara. He did not want to get caught up in in the crowd's anger. He thought about trying to persuade them to allow the boy to be banished and leave the valley immediately, but it was clear that madness had set in.

But he had not left even when the light began to leave the valley. Instead, he had looked for his friend, Ofyed, thinking to assist him in leaving. But when he arrived at Ofyed's tent, the tent flap had already been sewn shut and the stoning had begun.

He forced his way through the crowd and stood before them, trying to protect the tent.

"Stop! Dheren Ofyed has always dealt justly. He does not deserve this."

They froze, many with rocks in their hands ready to throw. One man whose hair had loosened and fell about his face like an uncombed tail, hefted a large stone from hand to hand.

"He allowed the dhavara in and brought ostuda upon us," the man shouted. Then he pointed at Neiren. "Seize this dheren. He should be next."

"No. No, Heilyn," another man said. "This dheren spoke against the dhavara. He tried to stop it. Let him be."

Heilyn turned and hurled the stone into the center of the tent. A guttural cry went up. The sound broke the small hold Neiren had had on the them and the stones began to fly once again.

One hit Neiren on the shoulder and he fell awkwardly.

The man who had spoken for him helped him up.

"It would be best if you left," he suggested. "They may soon care little that you tried to deny the dhavara. All dheren are suspect and most do not know you."

Then someone held a torch to the tent and it ignited quickly.

The crowd cheered.

Heavyhearted, Neiren returned to his horses, grateful for his life and that of his family. But, instead of leaving the valley as a wise man would do, he walked through the valley seeking out the other dheren. Even after finding dheren after dheren sewn into burned tents, he continued, hoping to be in time to save at least one. But he was too late. He looked around at the carnage, unable to think what to do next.

"We must leave," his wife urged. "Ayna'al fills the valley and we could all be next. If you will not leave for yourself, think about your children and servants. They do not deserve to die at the hands of this madness."

Neiren looked at the family around him and reason began to return. He bowed his head in defeat.

"You speak truly," he said.

His horse master led them to the far side of the valley where they could stay far away from the violence.

By the time they reached the southern pass and were safely out of the valley, he was exhausted. By then, many of the Dhervina had begun fleeing the valley and there were plenty of torches to light the way.

"What now?" his wife asked as they rode. "Will you continue as dheren?"

"I don't know," he said, his heart feeling like an anvil.

"If this is what happens when people don't like the decisions you make, then perhaps it is time to leave this to another."

"Who else is there now?" he asked.

He would wait for the rest of his kereit at the first stopping place. Perhaps by the time the others arrived, he would know what to do. But thousands of summers of tradition and knowledge had been obliterated and he truly feared what might now come to take its place.

The Kheran

The Kheran watched as the healer bent over Brys' inert form.

"She lives," the healer said finally. "But barely."

"Can she make the journey?" The Kheran knew she had to make a decision. It was a hard decision as the girl had just become Khutulun.

The healer shrugged. "It may be close," she said. "Her blood is very slow and I cannot hear her heart."

The Kheran looked at Brys again. She was about to order a measure of nightshade when her gaze fell on the medallion. Only a curve of it was visible, but it was enough.

"She will come with us," the Kheran said. "Give her the healing drought to send her to the land of shadows. They gave her the Khuriyat Khitan. If she truly is the Khevira, then they will heal her."

The healer bowed her head once and prepared the draught.

When it was ready, the two women made sure the entire measure made its way down Brys' throat. Then they lashed her to the litter.

The Kheran put Idris and the others of her tent in charge of the litter.

Then they began the long ride east.

GERAINT

When Geraint finally awoke, light from outside was filtering into the cave. It had to be well past dawn as it was light enough to see inside the cave.

He immediately looked around the cave, hoping to see his sister, but only Rhian was sleeping there.

He closed his eyes, wanting nothing more than to return to the land of shadows. He had dreamed Brys was on a long journey, but she had told him in the dream that she would return someday.

But now he was awake. Now he had to face the truth. She had not come to the cave because she could not.

Needing to see what had happened, he rose. He wrapped the grass colored blanket around himself and crept out to where he could see the valley.

Geraint was fearful of what he would see, but what met his eyes was completely unexpected.

The valley was completely deserted.

Other than a number of smoking lumps from night fires, nothing else remained.

After gaping at the deserted valley for nearly a gallop, he dropped the blanket and returned to the cave.

"Rhian," he whispered. He went over to where she was sleeping and was about to touch her shoulder when she jerked to on her feet.

"Where are they?" she asked, looking around as if for a place to hide.

"Gone."

She stared at him.

"Come see." He hurried back out of the cave.

Like him, Rhian stared in disbelief.

"Where did they go?" she asked finally.

"Back to the Great Circle, most likely," he said. "But I have never heard of such a thing."

"Something must have happened," Rhian said. "But what could have caused them to leave like this?"

"Someone died," he said flatly, pointing to the smoldering piles. "Someone died during the Tanaiste and that is forbidden."

He stared for only a moment longer. "We have to go see."

"No." She blocked his path. "What if someone is still there? Then it will be you on that valley floor."

"There is no one there," he said. "I do not know how I know this, but it is true. And even if someone were there, I must see if my sister is the one who died. I cannot leave without knowing."

He looked at Rhian's stricken face and felt as if he had gained ten summers during the night.

"You do not have to come," he told her. "Stay in the cave and I will return for you when I am finished."

She sighed deeply and shook her head. Geraint was afraid she was going to try to stop him, but she merely picked up the discarded blanket.

"What kind of traveling companion would I be if I let you do this thing by yourself? We will go together."

She led the way to the cave and Geraint blessed whatever gods there were that had brought her to him. He knew it could not have been the Great Horse given everything that had happened.

"I only intended to liberate one horse from Yorath," Rhian told him as they packed the supplies onto the horses. "Thank the gods I took two."

He gave her a sidelong look as he dragged a basket over to her. "You were only going to take one? You would have had to walk."

She shrugged. "I knew he would not miss one. At least for some time. I was so afraid I would be caught before I could leave. But somehow I found myself taking two. I thought that with all the excitement, it would be a simple matter for even two horses to go astray. I knew Yorath would not take the time to count his horses until much later. And, as you say, I would have had to walk a great deal more than I would like."

"We will trade them for other horses once we get among the Duta'ut," he said. "They bear Yorath's mark. Should he decide to search for you, it will be easy to find you by looking for the horses."

She stopped work for a moment, looked at the horses and then at Geraint. "Ahh. Very wise, Geraint of Halaka. I see we will travel well together."

Riding back into the valley felt strange. He had only ever been here when it was full of tents and people. Now it was empty and the ground was nearly bare of grasses. The valley somehow seemed smaller now that it was deserted.

"I was taught that the sacred valley should only be entered during the Tanaiste," he told Rhian as they rode in. "It feels strange with no one here."

"It is only a valley," she said. "You will see may more on your journey."

"That may be, but there is power here. I am just now of age, so there are things I can sense that I could not before. So I do not know if this feeling is usual. But there was death here and we should be gone before the sun dips below Khurtagin." He pointed to the mountain peak on the western edge of the valley.

She looked around the valley. "I agree."

They rode over to where Geraint's tent had stood.

The tent was still smoldering and he stared at the blackened remains.

"My father's bow was in there." It was the first thing that came to him. He didn't want to think about what else had been in there.

Then he saw the red ribbon. It fluttered in the slight breeze just beyond the charred remains of his family's tent. Most of it had burned, but there was enough to catch his eye.

He dismounted and walked over. When he bent down to pick it up, he saw the emblem of the snake that Brys had received when she pledged Khutulun.

He held it in his hand and closed his eyes, remembering how she had looked the last time he had seen her.

He felt Rhian's hand on his shoulder and opened his eyes, only then wiping away the tears.

"This was hers," he said. "She was so happy that she could finally become Khutulun."

"My heart is saddened for you," she said. "She was very brave."

He nodded. "Yes she was."

He looked back at the tent. "It will be difficult to bury them."

"If you move it or do anything else, they will know you are alive and may try to find you and kill you," Rhian said. "They did not die so you can throw your life away. To do so would dishonor their memory. Leaving them will be a reminder of the terrible thing they did this day. My people believe that those who are murdered and left unburied will take revenge on those who killed them. Give them shelter once you and they have had revenge."

He thought about it, but could not see another solution. They had none of the implements or ceremonial supplies needed. And he did not want to leave the tents open to the animals who would come.

He pinned the emblem and bit of ribbon to his vest, then looked at the tent. He did not know if her spirit could hear him, but made his pledge anyway.

"I will wear this until you are avenged," he promised in a loud voice thick with tears. "I will make them pay. No matter how long it takes. I will destroy all of them for what they have done. Then I will return here and return this emblem to you so you can wear it as you ride with the Great Horse in the lands that only see the time of summer."

He looked at the rest of the valley.

"I want to see the others."

Rhian helped him mount his horse and they rode to see which other tents had burned.

At the first, Geraint looked down and recognized the emblem.

"This was a dheren's tent," he said, shocked. The dheren were held in the greatest respect. To kill a dheren was worse than ayna'al. It was punishable by death.

"Was he still in there?" Rhian asked.

Geraint nodded and pointed. "You can still see where the flap was sewn shut."

He rode off to see the others. In each instance, the burned tent belonged to a dheren.

Geraint's stomach felt sour, as if he had just swallowed something that had gone rotten and wanted to spit itself out.

He stopped counting when he reached fifteen.

"Why would they burn the tents of the dheren?" Rhian's face was knotted in confusion. "Do they not decide the law?"

"Yes. But they confirmed me as full Dhervina," Geraint told her.

She looked around at all the burned tents. "Even my gods would weep at this."

"Yes."

She rode closer. "It was not your doing."

Geraint didn't say anything, but his thoughts were dark. *If not his fault, then where to lay the blame? It had all happened because of him.*

He clicked to his horse and rode on to the next tent and then the next. And on and on until he had seen them all.

He rode back to the remains of his family.

"This was the Tanaiste," he said. "No blood was to be shed here. No conflict was to occur. No death was to be caused."

He looked down at the burned tent and thought about his mother's beautiful carpets and his father's bow that were now gone. He thought about how comfortable their tent had been and how happy he had been here. He remembered his father's quiet manner and the way his mother always kissed him and told him that all would work out well when he was finally of age.

And how much she loved to gossip and how happy she was when he had told her about Andras' alliance with a kereit of Kypchak Ulsyn so she could be the first to tell.

And then he thought about the last time he had seen Brys and the way her red ribbons had looked in her black hair.

His tears blinded him and he looked away, unable to bear the thought of them dying in their tent because of him.

He looked back at the smoking valley one last time, searing the image into his mind.

Finally he looked at Rhian who waited patiently a few paces away.

"What do we do now?" he asked.

"We will travel together for a time," Rhian tells him. "There are many things I will teach you and we can protect each other until we find a safe place to stop.

He nodded. "That would be good," he said, remembering what Seren had told him. "If I am to destroy the Dhervina, there is much I need to learn."

BRYS

Brys stood on the plain in the land of shadows. She did not know how long she had been standing there, but she knew she had to start walking soon if she was to reach the cave in time.

It seemed a long journey. The mountains never seemed to get any closer even though she must have walked many gallops.

The sun hung directly overhead and never moved. She was hot and the heat made sweat run down her face and body as if she was standing in the rain. She realized she was terribly thirsty.

She thought about the pool she had found the last time she had visited this place and suddenly she was kneeling by its side.

She scooped up the water and drank. It felt marvelous cool and soothed her throat. She put some on her face to cool herself. Then she stepped into the pool and submerged herself, letting the heat drain out.

When she felt cool once again, she left the pool and walked to the cave, noticing that her clothing had already dried.

The old woman was still there. She looked up when Brys entered and got up from the stone hearth.

"Why are you here?" the old woman demanded. "You should not be here again like this."

"I do not know," Brys said. "I found myself on the plain and now I am here."

The old woman came over and placed her hand on Brys' forehead, then her cheek and finally her throat.

"Ahh."

"What is it?" Brys asked.

The old woman did not reply. She walked over to a ledge and poured something in a mug, then brought it back to Brys.

"You have been ill," she said. "Drink this and you will return home. Then you must return in life as quickly as you can."

"But how will I know how to find you?"

"Ask the Kheran," the woman said. "Now drink."

She helped lift the mug to Brys' lips.

Brys drank.

It was like drinking liquid honey. It was so sweet it brought tears to Brys' eyes.

Then she opened her eyes and saw nothing but sky above her. She could not remember what she had been doing or why she was now lying here. She tried to lift her head, but found she could not move. As best as she could tell, she was tightly bundled and strapped to some kind of litter which swayed and bumped.

A woman wearing a red cloak was riding alongside. She looked down at Brys and smiled.

Brys didn't know her, but the smile reassured her and she let herself fall back to sleep.

End Note

I had begun writing the Purgatory series and then stopped when I realized how important Geraint is to the story. I knew I had to write about him first so you would know who he was and why he plays the part he does.

In the writing, the story became much bigger than I had anticipated. And much better.

And it has given the Purgatory series a story arc that was ever so much better than what I had originally envisioned.

For more information about my books, please visit my website at www.KieranMcKendrick.com.

Finally, kudos to Soheil Toosi, the cover designer who created such a gorgeous cover for me. You can see more of his work at http://soheiltoosi.daportfolio.com.

KIERAN MCKENDRICK